The Lost Trail

John Tanner is returning home after serving two years in prison for shooting a man – but he pleaded guilty only to protect the young and pretty Becky Canasta, whose finger actually pulled the trigger.

Now John arrives home to find that Becky's father has had his safe looted and all of his savings taken. Moreover, the robbers have taken Becky!

Desperate to find her, John begins his quest in pursuit of the outlaws. News is out about the lost treasure and dozens of men are on the trail, battling with John to be the first to the riches. But for John there is something much greater at stake – the treasure is his only clue to Becky's whereabouts and her part in the robbery. Treachery and violence do not deter John – he will follow the trail to Hell if that is what it takes. . . .

The Lost Trail

Logan Winters

A Black Horse Western

ROBERT HALE · LONDON

© Logan Winters 2011
First published in Great Britain 2011

ISBN 978-0-7090-9110-3

Robert Hale Limited
Clerkenwell House
Clerkenwell Green
London EC1R 0HT

www.halebooks.com

Typeset by
Derek Doyle & Associates, Shaw Heath
Printed and bound in Great Britain by
CPI Antony Rowe, Chippenham and Eastbourne

ONE

Through the thin mountain mist the stars were only silver scars lingering from the hard battle that the settling night had waged against the sweltering day. John Tanner's gray horse waded on through the mist spread across the mountain flank, its hoofs silent against the damp pine needles. Did the horse have a memory of the trail? Tanner wondered. If it did, there was no indication of it in its plodding, methodical motion. Maybe horses are not burdened by remembrances of death and destruction. Having no memory of what once was they could not be fearful of the repetition of pain.

Tanner, however, recalled the past too well – yet he, only half as smart as his horse, was returning to Knox to offer his body and soul up on the altar of retribution. He shook his head and half-grinned ironically. A man long alone on the trail can fall into strange conversations with himself.

He found himself now six days out of Kansas City, only a morning away from the town of Knox where two years before. . . .

The pale moon lifted itself slowly from its eastern bed and rose higher, appearing like a pocked, leering skull as Tanner left the bunkhouse, walking to the gazebo set away from the house among the oak trees. The night altered its aspect as he neared the cone-topped building; the moon itself seemed to alter, becoming a golden promise riding high in the summer sky. Once he saw Becky he could hear the night birds singing in the willows along the creek. The moon, he decided, wore many faces.

Becky Canasta was wearing white and with her slender figure and long pale hair she was a quite angelic apparition as she stood in the gazebo waiting for Tanner. She did not turn her head at the sound of his approaching footsteps, but continued to lean on the railing of the structure, her eyes on unimaginable distances.

She was a girl to whom the night, the future held indefinable yet wonderful promise. When Tanner appeared at the foot of the steps leading up to the gazebo, he removed his hat and stood for a moment, overwhelmed by her quiet beauty.

'Hello,' Becky said softly as her eyes lifted to John Tanner.

There seemed some hesitation in her voice, a hint of fear in her eyes. Something Tanner did not understand, but which was obviously troubling her. He walked up the wooden steps of the gazebo and tried to fold her into his arms as he had at every opportunity since their first meeting on the C-bar-C Ranch, at the first indication that she had feelings for him as well – how could fortune have delivered such a gift to him? He was not rich, only a hard-working cowhand. He was not the sort you consider unusually handsome, but he seemed to suit Becky well enough, and that was all that mattered.

She held herself at a little distance from him and the troubled look remained in her eyes. Tanner lifted her chin and asked, 'What is it, Becky?'

'I can't tell you,' she replied, her lip trembling slightly. She held a small reticule in her hands. Now she turned away and twisted its tie-strings nervously.

'You can, you know. You can tell me anything, Becky.'

Then Tanner caught a moving shadow out of the corner of his eyes and she didn't have to tell him anything. Matt Doyle was stalking toward them, his eyes wide with rage.

'Didn't I tell you to stay away from that man!' Matt Doyle shouted, and he started up the steps of the gazebo.

Becky turned toward him with a pistol she had taken from her reticule and shot the man twice in the chest. Matt Doyle reeled back and slid down the steps on his back as lanterns were lit in the big house and the bunkhouse. Already a few men, drawn by the shots were rushing toward them through the oak trees.

Becky was trembling. Matt Doyle lay dead at the foot of the steps.

'What will I do!' she sobbed as boot steps came nearer.

'Give me that,' Tanner ordered and she meekly handed him the pistol she had fired, its barrel still warm. By the time the body of men rushed from the trees toward them, Tanner was standing over Matt Doyle, the pistol in his hand.

What else could he have done? Let Becky go to prison?

Tanner only received a two-year sentence because Becky Canasta had convinced judge and jury that he was protecting her from Matt Doyle. Still, the judge, noting that Matt Doyle had been unarmed, pronounced sentence, saying that he could not simply let Tanner go free.

The next two years. . . .

Becky quit writing a long time ago. Now he was back. There was no telling what kind of reception he would meet with.

Cresting out the pine-clad knoll he was able to look down on the C-bar-C now shrouded in low clouds. The main house was painted a dark green which almost matched the color of the surrounding trees. The bunkhouse and other outbuildings – except the barn which was bright red – were white-washed and weathered. There were a dozen or so horses in the corral and three hitched in front of the bunkhouse.

Of the gazebo Tanner could see nothing through the trees.

He waited, breathing shallowly, having no idea what sort of welcome he would receive. The gray horse shuddered and stamped a hoof impatiently, perhaps smelling the other horses and hay ahead. Tanner stroked the big gray's neck and started winding his way down through the timber, a man returning to the scene of his crime.

Reaching flat ground he started his horse imme-diately toward the main house, not knowing how Ben Canasta would greet him; if Becky were there, she would certainly welcome him, knowing what he had done for her. If everyone else on the ranch or

9

in town misunderstood the killing of Matt Doyle, she certainly knew, and knew that Tanner had paid the penalty for her crime.

That might not be enough to make her love him, but he would find out.

The ranch yard was quiet, except for one old yard man Tanner did not recognize. He swung down in front of the big green house, looped his reins around the hitch rail and started up the steps leading to the porch. He paused uncertainly at the door before knocking, but finally, with a deep sigh, did rap his knuckles on it.

It was a long time opening. Tanner could hear the slow shuffling steps approaching. They seemed hesitant, uncertain. Certainly it was not the welcoming he had imagined – with Becky rushing to greet him, perhaps throwing her arms around his neck with joy. That was the trouble with daydreams – eventually they collided with reality.

The door creaked open and a face Tanner should have known but found difficult to recognize peered out. It was an old face, weighed down with sorrow, it seemed. It flickered with surprise and a few words creaked from its lips.

'John Tanner!' the weak voice said. Now John recognized the man, though how he could have aged so much in a brief two years was a puzzle. Or maybe two years at the end of life are as short as they seem long in childhood.

'It's me, Mr Canasta,' John said to the ranch owner.

'Well, well,' the old man said, swinging the door wide. 'Come in, son. Come on in!' There was a real welcome in his words, but little strength behind them. Ben Canasta, it seemed, was fading rapidly.

Tanner followed Canasta through the entryway, through the living room where no fire burned in the fireplace despite the chill of the night. The room had a disused feel about it. They walked to Canasta's office which Tanner remembered well. Small, cluttered, with a tall window looking out at the grassland and the pine-shrouded hills beyond. This room, too, seemed almost neglected. There was a clutter of papers and folders on the desk and on the bookcase to the side, but it seemed to be old clutter, not the careless confusion scattered around by a busy man.

'Sit down, John,' Canasta was saying. He himself looked as if he could no longer hold himself upright as he sagged into the green-leather uphol-stered office chair behind his desk. 'It's fine to see you; I'm glad you came back,' Canasta said as he pointlessly stacked some of the papers on his desk with pale, crab-like hands. 'I hope they weren't too rough on you up there.'

'No, not really,' John said, as if it were a simple thing to rise before dawn and march in leg irons to the quarry at New Mexico Territorial Prison and swing a twelve-pound sledge hammer for ten hours a day under the raging sun, making small rocks out of big ones. There was no point in telling Canasta about all of that, and Tanner wanted to forget it himself.

'How's everything around here?' he asked the old man. It didn't seem possible, but Canasta's frown deepened still more.

'Becky's gone,' Canasta said. Tanner felt his heart twitch a little.

'Gone? You mean she moved into town, or got married? Something like that?'

'They stole her away,' Canasta said, his voice breaking badly. 'Held me up, robbed my safe and took her off with them.'

'When?' Tanner asked.

'Four days ago.'

The day before Tanner had been released from prison! 'Who did it, Ben? Tell me all about it.'

Ben Canasta nodded weakly as if his scrawny neck could barely support the weight of his head and the burden he carried. 'There was three of them, all wearing masks, and they pushed Becky into the

12

room with their guns drawn. They told me to open the safe – I wasn't going to argue with them, not while they held Becky under their guns. I gave them everything in there, including the money from the sale of this year's herd.

'They told me not to try following, not to call the law on them or something could happen to Becky. Then they took her and the money and were gone.'

'You've no idea who it was?' Tanner asked, feeling a cold fury beginning to grow in his chest. *Becky*? In the hands of gunmen.

'Of course I do!' Canasta said more strongly. 'It had to be someone who knew the workings of this ranch, didn't it? The following day there were three men missing from the bunkhouse – and it was two days before payday! I suppose that's not enough proof for a court, but it was enough for me.'

'Who were they? Would I remember them?' Tanner asked.

'One of them was a new-hire named Charlie Cox, one was Wes Dalton – you might remember him. Their leader was Morgan Pride – I know you recall him.'

'Yes, I do,' said Tanner, having a vivid memory of the dark-eyed, broad-shouldered man with the narrow mustache who had tried more than once to badger Tanner into a fistfight over trivial matters.

Dalton he barely remembered, except to recall that he was a sallow, silent blond who never put in a day's work if he could help it.

'What can I do to help, Ben?' Tanner asked.

'Get Becky back for me,' Ben Canasta asked, lifting his watery eyes in a plea to Tanner. 'John, I don't think I'm long for it. My health's been failing. I need to know that my daughter's safe; I need to have her brought home to me.'

'Surely the hands. . . .'

'We possed up at first, but those thieves had it in mind to ride long and hard. They each took an extra horse from my string and lit out across the desert. Three days it was we chased them, but the sun grew hotter, the land wilder. I knew the boys had lost their will to pursue them. Then we lost their trail up in the red-rock hills. There wasn't anything more to be done. Besides the ranch needed to be tended to. If I could have gone on by myself, I would have, but I just couldn't, John.' Now his deeply concerned frown returned. 'Maybe thirty years ago, twenty even, but now. . . .'

'I'll give it my best try, Ben,' Tanner told him. 'Give me an idea of where you lost the trail and I'll start from there – we'll talk later,' he added, noticing that the old man was now having difficulty staying alert. The weight of his sorrows, the guilt he felt over not being able to find Becky were a lot for him to carry. Tanner turned and started toward the door, trying to frame a plan in his mind.

'Dine with me tonight, John,' Canasta said. 'After a nap, I'll have more strength to go over all this.'

John just nodded, a gesture Ben Canasta probably did not see. John believed that the old man had fallen asleep at his desk.

John Tanner went out into the corridor and began making his way toward the front door. He was nearly to it when a side door of the corridor opened and he was confronted by a small dark-eyed woman wearing a neat black dress with white lace at the neck and cuffs. Tanner knew her – Ben Canasta's housekeeper. She was on the young side of thirty but acted much older.

'Oh,' was what she said, but not in the way a person does when surprised. There was something approaching disgust in her voice, at least distaste. She puckered her mouth so that small vertical lines appeared on her upper lip and her dark eyes flared.

'Hello, Monique.'

'I thought we'd seen the last of you. I'd hoped so,' the housekeeper said.

'Not yet,' Tanner replied. 'There's several things that still have to be straightened out. For instance, Ben wants me to have a try at finding Becky.'

15

'She's gone,' the housekeeper said, stepping nearer to look up into John Tanner's eyes. 'And we're all the better off for it. Even Mr Canasta, though he doesn't realize it yet.'

'I don't think so – I think the old man is dying and he needs his daughter around the house.'

'Why? I see to Mr Canasta's needs. Better than his daughter ever could.'

Tanner shifted his feet and turned his hat in his hands. Monique's anger was obvious, but not who or what she was so angry with.

'What do you know about the robbery?' he asked and her face tightened still more.

'Nothing – it happened, that's all I know. But I have an opinion: Becky was behind it!'

Tanner shook his head, not believing the hatred in those black eyes. 'That makes no sense,' he said. 'Becky will fall heir to everything her father owns. The ranch, cash money – everything. Why would she plot to rob him?'

'Because that's the way she is! She wants every-thing and she wants it when she wants it. She doesn't like to wait. She's behind it, I promise you.' Then Monique bowed her head into her palms and sobbed. 'She just takes things,' Monique blubbered, 'like she tried to take Matt Doyle from me.'

That was a stunner, if true. But it could not be,

could it. Monique had loved the dead cowboy, but he had been pursuing Becky? Things like that did happen, of course, but if it was true that Becky had loved Matt Doyle in return, why had she killed the young man? John Tanner shook his head. It had been a very long day and he had a long ride ahead of him. He needed a good night's sleep just then more than anything else. Monique was a jilted, hysterical woman, nothing more.

Without another word he nodded, made his way out the door and into the chilly, foggy night. When he glanced back, Monique was still standing in the doorway, arms folded beneath her breasts, staring out at him, the night or at lost dreams.

It was chilly and so after putting his horse up in the barn, which took no more than a half an hour even with pitching hay down from the loft for the gray to munch on, he walked across the yard, passing through the oak-shadows, to the bunkhouse which was lighted but strangely silent. There was usually a lot of joking, teasing in bunkhouses as the hands prepared for bed. There was none at all on this night.

Just as he stepped up on to the porch, Tanner caught a glimpse of a shadow flitting away between buildings to disappear among the trees. A woman in black, her dark hair now loose around her shoulders. Monique, who else could it be?

Opening the door to the bunkhouse Tanner stepped into a wall of silent resentment. Men sat at the low tables or on their bunks, watching with angry eyes as Tanner entered. Matt Doyle's killer had returned.

The man who came forward to meet John Tanner was named Ted Everly. A big red-headed man who had lost a lot of hair in the last two years and now appeared to have a monk's cap. Time had done nothing, however, to diminish the massive shoulders and deep chest of Everly, nor the cutting gaze of his gray-blue eyes. Everly planted himself in front of Tanner, hands on his hips and said:

'You're not wanted here, Tanner.'

'I work here,' John replied, watching as some of the hands began to gather in a knot. 'Ben Canasta just took me on.'

'It doesn't matter,' Ted Everly said, stepping even nearer, his eyes losing none of their threatening expression. 'I don't want you here, Tanner. None of us does. You can either get out now, or I promise you you will never leave – not alive.'

TWO

Tanner made his way to the barn across the yard where the oak trees cast moon shadows. Even with the thick ground fog he could find his way easily. The tall red structure was black against the starry skies. Riding farther on this night was unthinkable, no matter what Everly and the boys in the bunkhouse had strongly suggested. The last few days had left John Tanner trail-weary and sore.

Entering the barn he first saw that his horse still had enough water and feed, then climbed up a pole ladder into the hayloft. Pulling the ladder up after him, he formed a bed of hay in the farthest corner and lay down to fall into a heavy but troubled sleep.

Morning arrived far too early, the harsh glare of low sunlight cutting into the barn through the small loading window. Tanner sat up rubbing at his sleep-encrusted eyes, scratching at his arm where some small insect had bitten him half a dozen times. Then he lowered the flimsy ladder once more and descended with stiff muscles to the floor of the barn. The double doors to the barn were suddenly swung wide.

'I told you that his horse was still here,' a cowboy Tanner did not recognize said proudly. Ted Everly and three other hands stood there, silhouetted by the rising sun. Everly was glowering and he unbuttoned his sleeves to roll them back over his thick forearms.

'I told you to go, Tanner. I'm going to make you wish you had listened.'

With that, the bulky Everly crossed the straw-strewn floor of the barn, his broad face set with vengeful purpose. John Tanner could do nothing but wait, measuring his chances against the bull-like Everly. John's muscles had become nearly as solid as the rocks he had been breaking up at the Territorial Prison over the past two years, and even before that they had been as strong as five years working on the range could have made them. Still, Everly's chest was twice as thick as Tanner's, and he had at least fifty pounds of weight on him.

John Tanner didn't really like his chances – but there was nowhere to run.

He didn't wait for Everly to land the first blow. As soon as the big man was in range Tanner jabbed out with two straight left-hand shots, the first one drawing blood from Everly's nose, the second rocking his head back. Everly wiped a callused hand across his face, his expression not changing, and he came forward again, neck bowed, meaty fists held low, too low, Tanner thought, and so he feinted with his left and then arced a right-hand hook against Tanner's ear, stunning the big man, but only slightly. Blood flowed from his left ear, and now Everly who had yet to land a blow formed a savage, angry sneer with his thick lips. He bulled forward so that Tanner could not hold him off and slammed John up against the side of one of the stall partitions, pinning him there briefly before he took half a step back and began hammering away with lefts and rights, first going down to Tanner's ribs, then up to his head.

John was able to bob his head away from Everly's big fists just enough so that the blows bounced off the top of his skull. There was no dodging the body shots, and his ribs flared up with sudden fire. Knowing he had to get off the partition, John stepped down hard with his boot heel on Everly's toes and then brought his elbow up into Everly's nose, backing the big man up enough so that John could slide out into the middle of the barn floor. There his jabbing could be used more effectively, and he went back to it, throwing three straight left hand shots into the big man's face. One of these split Everly's eyebrow and blood began to seep from it into his right eye.

This might have gone on forever, John thought – he having the advantage in the open, the big cowman trying to find a way to drive him up against a partition to pound away at his body with his huge fists. John decided he had had enough. He dropped his right hand to his holster and drew his Colt .44, halting Everly in his tracks.

Everly looked surprised, perhaps even a little angry at ending a fight this way, but Ted Everly's face had taken a beating and John thought that perhaps the big man was happy to have the fight ended, in a way that did not damage his reputation as a fighter in front of the ranch hands.

'That's the coward's way out,' Everly snarled, his voice reflecting not injured pride so much as an attempt to save face.

'Maybe,' Tanner agreed, backing toward the stall where his gray horse stood watching without concern. 'I'm riding out anyway, Everly. Don't you understand – I'm not planning on staying around the C-bar-C, I never was. I only need to saddle my pony and have a last talk with Ben Canasta and then I'll be gone.'

Everly wiped more blood from his face and then grumbled one last threat. 'See that you are – or I'll be back.'

Then the big man spun on his heel and limped toward the barn doors, pausing to cast one evil backward glance at Tanner before he walked out into the bright new sunlight, his men following him toward the bunkhouse.

Tanner found that his hands were trembling as he fixed saddle blanket and saddle into place, lightened the cinches, slipped the gray its bit and led it out toward the big house. He should have just shot the bastard, he was thinking, but that would have led to the entire crew grabbing their guns and coming after him. There are no men more clannish than cowboys riding for the brand. Their loyalties are fierce, if often misplaced.

Tanner hitched his pony, glanced around seeing no one, and rapped on the door to the green house. Eventually Monique swung the door open. Her dark eyes searched his face and torn shirt with seeming satisfaction.

'Mr Canasta hasn't come down yet,' she said.

'I'll wait inside, if I may.'

'Think you're safer in here?' Monique asked.

'A little,' John said, slipping through the door before she could close it in his face. 'Have you any coffee?'

'I have,' she said without expression.

'Any chance of getting a cup?'

Monique only shrugged and turned away toward a door which he knew led into the kitchen. Tanner followed her. He sat at an undecorated oak wood table and watched the new sun cutting a bright pattern across the table and floor, interrupted only briefly by the dark shadow of Monique moving through the sun rays. She returned eventually with a white ceramic cup filled with steaming, black coffee. Monique went around the table and sat staring at him as he blew on the coffee, trying to cool it.

'They'll be back to finish the job, you know,' she said.

'I won't be here,' Tanner said. 'But why do they want to beat me up . . . why did you tell them to do it? I saw you last night, Monique.'

'Why?' She laughed. It was a brief, harsh sound in the back of her throat. 'Just because you gunned down the only man I've ever loved – Matt Doyle – and got off with only two years in prison? You take a guess, Tanner.'

'But, I didn't. . . .' John Tanner swallowed his

explanation. To tell the truth now would do nothing but expose Becky Canasta to prosecution – that would likely kill Ben. Besides, at this late date no jury would be likely to convict on Tanner's word alone, and he did not want Becky convicted. According to the law, the crime had been solved, the penalty paid. He wanted to tell Monique something to exonerate himself, but there was nothing that could be said. Even if she believed him – most improbable – she would transfer her fury to Becky. He could do nothing but fall silent, and sip at his coffee until Monique told him:

'Mr Canasta is coming downstairs now. You may as well go into his office. Take your coffee.'

'Should I take a cup to him?'

'Mr Canasta gave up coffee a few years ago,' Monique said.

Tanner made his remembered way back to Ben Canasta's office and found the old man standing at the window, hands behind his back. He was humming aimlessly to himself.

'Mr Canasta? It's Tanner, I've come back to finish our business.'

The humming broke off. Ben Canasta turned from the window to take his seat behind his desk.

'Did you sleep well?' Canasta asked.

'It wasn't the sleep, it was the waking up that went

hard,' Tanner said, and now Ben Canasta seemed to notice the torn shirt, the lump on John's forehead.

'I see,' Canasta said, thoughtfully.

'But we were going to talk about the trail you lost on the desert.'

'Yes, we were,' Ben said, folding his thin hands in front of him. 'We lost their sign up at Split Rock.' Which might have seemed like a vague description to someone unfamiliar with the area, but Split Rock was a landmark, some fifty feet tall which stood where three trails met. One leading to the town of Knox, not far distant, the other two forking off, south toward Ruidoso, and north toward Las Palmas. It was a well-known junction in this part of the country.

'Well,' Ben said wearily, 'you know how many people ride those trails – we had been following eight horses – four of them mounted, now there were tracks in all directions – hundreds of them. And the ground is deep in red sand over that way, as you know. There was no way of finding the trail again.'

'You still think that Morgan Pride is their leader?' Tanner asked.

'I know he is, damnit!' the old man said, banging a fist against his desk. 'A mask doesn't hide your face from someone who has known you twenty years.' Ben Canasta took a deep breath and leaned back in his chair. 'I took that man in when he was only a pup – this is the way he's repaid me.'

'I'll find him,' Tanner promised, though how he was going to do it remained a question.

'I don't care if you do or don't,' Canasta said. 'I suppose I don't really care about the money, either. But find Becky for me, Tanner. Just bring Becky home.'

Tanner walked out of the office, feeling low and beaten. His prospect of finding Becky Canasta was dim, and he knew it. His ribs ached; he was hungry; he was tired of the long-riding. Monique met him just as he crossed the living room toward the front door to the house.

'Are you riding now?' she asked with her eyelids half-lowered. She still wore black on this morning.

'I gave my word.'

'I think you may not be riding alone,' Monique said. 'I think there may be some men trailing behind you.'

'What are you telling me?' Tanner asked.

'Nothing,' she said with a small shrug, 'only that you cannot expect to be alone. And if you are so fortunate as to find Becky Canasta, I would leave her where you find her, because it would not be good for her if she shows up again and I am still here.'

Her eyes, now wide open glinted wildly. Perhaps Monique was not mad, but she was driven by hatred – of Becky who had stolen her man, Matt Doyle, and of John Tanner whom she believed had murdered him.

'I gave my word,' Tanner replied briefly. 'If you think that Ben Canasta would ever side with you against his own daughter, you are deeply mistaken.'

'If you think that troubles me, you are badly mistaken, John Tanner. I will be surprised if he is alive to see his daughter return. I will be surprised if the old man does not have a serious reversal while you are riding the long trail.'

Tanner stared at the dark woman; her threat was implicit, but was she making it to frighten Tanner, or was she capable of murder? Either way, John could do nothing about it. His decision had been made, and his course of action was clear. Find Split Rock and follow the lost trail wherever it might lead.

The rising sun was warm on Tanner's back as he left the wooded knolls and lined out toward Split Rock on the Apache Canyon trail, the route Ben Canasta would have taken. Of course at this late date there was no sign of the passing horses Morgan Pride and his men would have left behind. Tanner was riding on blind faith, wondering what impulse had led him to believe he could do what the posse on the heels of the robbers could not accomplish.

It was, of course, the only line of action possible. Becky had to be found and delivered to her father. Or was it only for him, Tanner wondered, as he remembered the girl in the moonlight. No matter, she could not be left in the clutches of three armed and desperate thugs.

He rode on as the day grew warmer. Once through the canyon, the land turned long, flat and floored with red sand. Ahead, already he could see the huge formation of Split Rock, he hurried on a little before forcing himself to remember that the huge boulder was not the end of his trail, but only the beginning.

And he was being followed. That was certain. Although he could not see them or estimate their numbers, there were riders behind him. On the desert flats, the dust rising from the hoofs of their horses was visible even at this distance.

Tanner's face was grim. Well, Monique had warned him – threatened him? that he would be followed. Monique did not want Becky to return to the ranch alive. Would these men actually kill the rancher's daughter? If so, what sort of plan did they have for John Tanner himself? It didn't take a lot of imagination. One more lost soul missing on the long desert. And to Monique's mind it would be the man who had shot down her lover, Matt Doyle, on that moonlit night so long ago.

The woman carried her grief well and long. Tanner rode on; there was no talking to Monique or the ranch hands. Only time could resolve this situation – if there was a resolution.

Who was back there, following him? Certainly Ted Everly who had developed a grudge against Tanner. There were too many other possibilities for the remainder of the trackers. John thought they were a small group of men, no more than three or four, judging by the amount of dust they created in their passing. It was enough to do the work they had agreed to do.

Split Rock was sweltering in the sunlight. The monument soared skyward, offering shade on its west side. The red behemoth was nevertheless too hot to touch. Tanner swung down from the saddle and loosened the twin cinches to give his gray horse some relief. Then he walked around the red granite boulder, noticing the residue of scores of campfire, seeing the hundreds of inscriptions carved in the rock by travelers, searching for some possible sign of Becky and her kidnappers.

It was impossible, and he knew it even before

beginning. Squatting on his heels in the warm shade he tried to logic it out. Tired men, weighed down with the wealth of their robbery riding weary horses – why would they not take the shortest route, the road to the town of Knox to regroup, re-equip and rest? That was what Tanner, himself, would have done, but that did not mean it was what Morgan Pride had done. The distant town of Ruidoso was an option, and the still more distant Las Palmas. But why not ride on on fresh, well-fed, watered ponies after spending a night in a Knox hotel, drinking some whiskey, eating a decent meal.

Tanner rose – they had gone into Knox, he felt sure. And so he would follow, riding through the heat of the day. He tightened his cinches again and swung aboard the trustworthy gray horse which was going to be used hard on this day, and probably for many days to come. Possibly he should trade it for a fresh animal in Knox, but that seemed something like abandonment. No matter – he would see first what he could turn up in Knox, the town he had been tried and convicted in for the shooting of Matt Doyle.

His homecoming would not be a warm one. He knew that there were not a few people in Knox who thought that he should have been hanged for killing Matt Doyle. Turning the gray's muzzle westward, he traveled on through the heat of the day, glancing back frequently to make sure that the men from the C-bar-C were not gaining on him.

The land now began to rise and fall. Small clumps of creosote cluttered the landscape and stands of mesquite cast lacy shadows across the red sand desert. If anything was living on the desert, Tanner saw none of them. If water had ever touched this sere land, there was no sign of it. No water-cut gullies creased the desert; there was no sign of ancient tinajas or seasonal ponds. There might not have been a tree standing for twenty or fifty miles.

At last, with the lowering sun beaming directly into his eyes as day began to sigh into darkness, Tanner caught a glimpse of Knox, a tiny settlement appearing like a group of matchboxes at this distance. It gave him a false sense of satisfaction to have made it this far; his horse was faltering slightly as he neared the town. His pursuers were no nearer.

Day settled into purple dusk as he rode along the main street of the small town. He glanced automatically at the hitched horses along the street although he had no idea what the kidnappers had been riding. There were a few weary ponies tied here and there, salt-streaked from a desert run, but that did not mean that Becky's kidnappers had ridden them. Tanner searched for a stable where his tired gray could be fed, watered and rested. It wasn't hard to find one. In fact two competing stables sat facing each other across the dusty main street. Flipping a coin mentally, Tanner chose the one on his left for no particular reason.

Swinging down from the saddle, he walked his horse in the open double doors of the stable and called out. After a minute a nearly hairless, Spanish-looking man appeared. Tanner had spent the time looking at the stabled horses.

'I was looking for a party with eight horses – four ridden, four spare – who might have come in here,' Tanner said. 'Three men and one woman. Have you seen them?'

'Are you a lawman?' the stable man asked in a deeply accented voice.

'No.'

'Then I don't see nothing,' the man said truculently.

'All right,' Tanner answered, seeing that he was not going to get anywhere with this one. Then he instructed the stable hand on how to grain his horse, something the sullen man listened to with disgust as if Tanner had impugned his knowledge of animals.

Arrangements made, Tanner went out into the near-darkness of the desert dusk and trudged across the street to the other stable. He might have more luck there. The stars were clear in the high sky. The moon had not yet made its debut. Somehow that lifted Tanner's spirits.

'Hello!' he tried at the stable door and after awhile a grubby little man, scratching at his pot belly came out of the shadows to meet him.

'Looking for some people,' Tanner said, repeating their description.

'No, sir,' the stable hand replied. 'Seen no one like that tonight – I would have remembered a young woman.' Then he leaned closer to Tanner in the lantern light and said, 'Say, aren't you. . . ?'

John had already turned to go. He seemed to vaguely remember the man. He may have been on the jury that had convicted Tanner of manslaughter. There would be others in Knox who would recognize him, he knew. He would not be welcome in their town. *Killer*. No matter, he decided. He had to find Becky and get her safely home for Ben Canasta's sake . . . and hopefully for his own. The moon had now begun rising slowly, seeming large and reddish-gold on the eastern horizon where red desert merged with dark skies. John turned his eyes down. He knew too much about the moon. It always showed a perplexing face.

The town of Knox was pretty much shut down for

the night. The storekeepers had gone home to their wives and kids. The bank was locked up tight. The night people had begun to emerge; the saloons were kicking in, ready for the rude onslaught of the drinkers, gamblers and brawlers.

John Tanner headed for the nearest bar – the long-riders would be wanting refreshment. John had long ago tired of the saloons, of the shouting, pushing, cursing and fighting, but his best hope of finding Morgan Pride and his men was to search them. What about Becky? Where would they have stashed her, women not being allowed in saloons – mainly for their own protection.

And what about the men on his backtrail – Ted Everly and whoever was riding with him? They were bound to catch up with him, and soon. With guns in front of him and guns behind him, Tanner was caught in a trap he had laid for himself.

He stepped from the boardwalk to pass toward the bright lights of the saloon beyond the alley. That was where they jumped him.

THREE

Passing, Tanner was jerked back into the alley by strong hands. There might have been three men waiting for him, possibly four. He didn't take the time to count. Each one of the men wanted his turn to hit John, though. He took three hammer-like blows to his ribs and three or four shots to his head. Fighting back in the darkness against an over-whelming foe was virtually impossible. The most he could do was hide his face behind his forearms, although once he did manage to drive a boot heel into one of their knees, causing the man to turn away cursing. That did not leave the final outcome in any doubt. The last Tanner knew was that someone had raised a club of some sort – or possibly it was a rifle stock – and driven it down against his temple and all of the lights across the world blinked out.

When he came to – was it minutes or hours later? – his muscles were stiff, his head was a throbbing mass of pain and he was cold, very cold beneath the starry night sky. Shivering, he took a deep, cautious breath which caused fiery pain to arc across his ribcage. Carefully he repositioned his body, first to enable himself to sit up and then to reach for the support of the unpainted wall fronting the alleyway.

Finally making his way upright, he stood dizzily listening to the boozy uproar from the nearby saloon, breathing carefully, trying to think.

Had that been Morgan Pride's gang, or the following band of men led by Ted Everly? There was no telling – it could have even been a group of local town toughs.

'Are you going to make it?' the voice behind him inquired. Tanner turned his head enough to see the woman – twenty or so years of age – watching him, a shawl thrown over her shoulders.

'Sure,' Tanner rasped.

'I don't think it's so sure,' she replied. 'If you can make it over here, come along inside.'

She turned and opened an unseen alley door, letting the light from within flood out.

With nowhere else to go, Tanner started that way,

moving stiffly, cautiously. He did not trust anyone in the town of Knox. Bent over at the waist, hand across his battered ribs, he went through the doorway and had it shut behind him. Looking around he found himself in some sort of ladies' hat shop with knick-knacks and laces scattered about. He leaned back against one of the counters and raised his eyes to see a dark-haired woman with shoulder-length tresses watching him with calm, concerned eyes. She continued to clasp the shawl tightly around her shoulders. Beneath that was a white blouse with a few frills decorating it, tucked into a dark blue skirt.

'What are you, a gambler?' she asked.

'No, why do you ask?'

'From time to time men try to settle accounts outside,' she said, nodding toward the alley.

'No, I'm no gambler. Did you recognize the men? See which way they went?'

'No and no,' she said with a rich laugh. 'I was closing up for the night when I peeked out and saw them going at you. When you went down, I called out, 'The marshal is on his way,' and they scattered. I shut my door and locked it right away.'

'Was the marshal on his way?'

'Of course not – how could I have notified him in a few minutes? Nevertheless, the threat of a man with a badge was enough to send them running.'

Tanner shifted his position slightly, still holding his ribs. 'I thank you for your help. Is the town marshal still McGraw?'

'Why, yes he is. Do you know him?'

'Not really.' Jack McGraw was the man who had arrested Tanner for the killing of Matt Doyle, spoken a few words to him in the town jail and escorted John to the courthouse for his trial. McGraw was not a cruel or judgmental man; he only took care of his own work and let the courts sort out the rest.

'I think. . . .' Tanner said wearily, then the world began to whirl around again and he felt his knees begin to buckle. He fell face forward against the hard wooden floor of the shop, and the world vanished again from before his eyes.

Someone was humming a little tune melodically. The sun was bright through the pink curtains on the south wall. Tanner was in a bed with pink ruffles and a canopy. But where was he and why was he there? His nose itched and he moved one arm automatically to scratch it. The motion caused jagged pain to jolt through his ribcage and he remembered. He had been beaten in an alley and an unknown woman had come to his rescue. He had passed out on her floor and somehow she, or someone else, had managed to drag him into this bedroom where he now lay, squinting into the glare of morning sunlight.

He was in the town of Knox pursuing Becky Canasta, and by now his enemies had had time to gather and ride away while he could do nothing but lay in a pink bed, feeling sorry for himself.

'I was wondering when you would wake up,' the dark haired girl at the doorway said. She entered, carrying a silver tray with two cups and a coffee pot on it. 'I'm sorry for not sending for the doctor, but a lot of men in your situation would not want one.'

'What situation is that?' he asked, as she towed a small round table to his bedside and he tried to wedge himself into a sitting position.

'Oh, I don't know,' she answered, pouring coffee into two small cups painted with flowers, seating herself in a blue velvet covered chair. 'Men with troubles.'

'I'm not an outlaw,' he said, managing to reach out far enough to pick up one of the small cups by its seemingly fragile ear. 'If that's what you meant. The thing is,' he confessed after a short sip of the hot coffee, 'well, my name is John Tanner.'

'My name is Candice Moore,' the unperturbed woman said as if John's words were meant only as an introduction. Her eyes searched his battered face; Tanner fingered his eyes – still sleep-encrusted He tugged at an eyelash.

'You haven't been here long have, you?' he asked.

'More than a year,' she answered, sipping at her own cup of coffee.

'What I am talking about happened before you got here – two years ago to be exact.'

'Do you want to tell me about it?' Candice asked.

'It's something I never wanted to tell anybody about – not all of it, anyway.'

'I have the time,' Candice said. 'Business is not exactly booming – and there is a bell over the door. Besides,' she added with a smile. 'You aren't going anywhere right now. Why not let me play confidante?'

Why not? Tanner thought. He had been carrying his burden alone for a long time and Candice seemed receptive. A small, dark woman with a bright smile which only broke out now and then, and intent greenish eyes which reflected concern and puzzlement alternately as Tanner told her the truth about the murder of Matt Doyle and its aftermath which led up to his beating in the alley.

'It's a wonder they didn't kill you,' she said after one of Tanner's long pauses.

'I think they would have – if not for you. They just

didn't want to bring attention to themselves with gunfire.'

Candice was thinking along a different line. 'Two years of your life,' she said at length. She leaned slightly forward, hands clasped between her knees. 'Did you love her that much, Tanner?'

It was a woman's question, of course – one of the things they are always thinking about. He answered with a shake of his head:

'I don't know now. It seemed so.'

'You may have been just used. Duped.'

'I know it,' he admitted.

'Then why. . . ?'

'I have to take Becky home for her father's sake. Maybe when I see her, I'll know if I'm over her. I just don't know.'

'I think,' Candice said rising, smoothing out her skirt, 'that you are a noble man, John Tanner.' She scooped up the tray and the cups and went out. A few seconds later John could hear the small bell over the shops door tinkling, hear Candice welcoming a customer. He lay back in the wide pink bed.

Noble? Foolish, maybe. Infatuated – clinging desperately to a vision of a woman in white shimmering in the moonlight. But noble? He doubted it. He was only a man who had accepted a challenge and was committed to following through to its conclusion.

He owed that much to Ben Canasta and to Becky.

Tanner lay back and closed his eyes. He heard the ping of a cash register and then the door over the bell tinkling again as the customer went out of the shop. Then there was the sound of Candice's leather heels crossing the floor toward the room where he lay. Tanner feigned sleep. He could not have said why, except that he felt he had done enough talking for one morning. The door to the bedroom opened again and then closed silently. Candice was gone, and Tanner felt a vague sense of loss and guilt. It was all for the better – the girl was young and did not need to be dragged further into his problems. As soon as he was able, he was leaving. Knox had never been a lucky town for him.

The trouble was that after an entire morning and evening spent in bed, barely moving, Tanner could tell that he was not going to be in shape to ride the long desert for quite a while. Sometime later as dusk had begun to settle, Candice returned with a lantern, bringing with her a young doctor with a pinched face who made John sit up straight as he bound his ribs tightly – very tightly.

'As you probably know there's no real treatment for healing broken ribs,' the doctor said as he worked. 'Except remaining still. You should stay in this bed – or another – for a day or so. A week would be better. You will still hurt, but it will improve your chances of the bones mending and not splintering to puncture a lung.'

Tanner knew that was right, but he was already weary of being bed-ridden. There were only a few positions he could find which did not intensify the misery he was enduring, and to shift between these required painful movements.

He tried to raise anger against the men who had beat him in the alley, but it was hard to do. It's not easy to sustain an anger against an unknown enemy.

The door opened again and Candice appeared there, dressed in yellow. She peered at him out of the shadows.

'Do you want to try to eat something? The doctor said it wouldn't do any harm for you to walk as far as my kitchen – though it will cause you some discomfort.'

'I'll try,' Tanner said. Then he gestured. 'I don't have a shirt on, though.'

'I'm a pretty informal girl,' Candice smiled. 'Need help getting up?'

'I don't,' Tanner said, struggling and failing to place his legs over the side of the bed. 'I suppose I do,' he admitted.

With Candice's help he made it to his feet and

she led him down a narrow corridor to the kitchen beyond where the good aroma of food cooking caused his belly to tighten. When was the last time he had eaten? When was the last time he had actually enjoyed a home-cooked meal?

Candice helped Tanner to sit in a wooden chair and apologized, 'I'm sorry – I don't have much around the house just now. I made fatback in white beans, mustard greens and cornbread.'

'Sounds good to me,' Tanner said honestly. While he waited to be served he watched the slender back of the girl in the yellow dress, listened to the small sounds she made as she dished the food out. At another time, in another place. . . .

But now this was the town of Knox and as soon as he was half-well he meant to ride out on to the long desert again.

Candice seated herself opposite him and they both ate in relative silence. The food was simple, but warm and good. Still when Tanner could eat no more, there was half of his dinner left untouched. Candice frowned at his plate.

'I'm sorry, I told you it wasn't much,' she said.

'It's not that – it's just that I don't have my appetite back yet.'

'I'll try to find something special for breakfast,' Candice said, still looking as if she had failed him.

'That's right – I will have to stay here until breakfast, I suppose.' He hesitated. 'I'm sorry to be putting you out like this. Here I am, a stranger, sleeping in your bed.'

'It's nothing,' Candice said without looking up from her plate. 'Nothing at all.'

Back in bed Tanner pondered the woman's last words and decided that she had meant only what she had said: It was nothing at all.

It was two full days and nights before Tanner felt he had to try to travel on, before he felt strong enough to even attempt it. Candice helped him dress – pulling on his shirt was impossible to do alone. The shirt was a new one with blue and white checks that Candice had bought for him. She watched as he buttoned it up and stood looking at his bruised face in the bedroom mirror. Twice she seemed ready to say something, but held her voice. After Tanner had managed – clumsily – to sling his belt gun around his hips and buckle it, Candice slipped out of the room as Tanner made his way toward the front door of the shop.

When she returned he saw that she was holding his gray Stetson.

'I found it in the alley. I brushed it and had it blocked.'

'It looks better than ever,' John said, meaning it.

Candice handed it to him as if she were giving up something very important.

'If I ever get back this way. . . .' he began.

'Oh go on and get yourself killed!' she said sharply. Tanner turned and opened the door, causing the little bell to tinkle. Candice stepped quickly near him. 'I'm sorry,' she said. 'I don't know what came over me.' He smiled and she stuck out a small hand for him to shake, then changed her mind, went to tiptoes and kissed him lightly on the lips.

She rushed away, her eyes moist. Tanner watched her for a moment, then stepped out of the door into the bright desert sunlight.

'Well, you never know,' he muttered to himself. Then he halted on the plankwalk, standing in the narrow band of shade cast by the awning and considered. What now? He still had not searched the town for Morgan Pride and his gang, for Becky.

He had started toward the stable to see to his horse when he nearly walked into the last man in Knox that he wanted to see. He was tall, bulky and the morning sunlight reflected off the silver badge he was wearing. Marshal Jack McGraw planted himself in front of John Tanner, his thumbs hooked into his gun belt. He looked Tanner up and down, his eyes alert but clouded.

47

'I thought it was you,' McGraw said. 'What are you doing in this town, Tanner? You know it might not be too healthy a place for you to visit.'

'I'll be leaving soon. I was trying to find some friends.'

'Looks like someone already told you what Knox thinks of you,' McGraw said. John reflexively reached up and touched the knot on his head, his black eye.

'I was looking for Becky Canasta,' John said 'and I got jumped.'

'Becky Canasta? Does Ben know you're still bothering that girl.'

'He's the one who sent me,' John said defensively. 'We think Becky has been kidnapped, and those who took her are the ones who beat me up.'

'It's more likely that it was people who remembered you as the man who killed Matt Doyle. A lot of folks think you got off too easy, Tanner. At any rate, Becky Tanner has not been in town – I'd have seen her.'

'All right, if you say so,' John said. 'I mean to have another look around, though. Just to be sure.'

Jack McGraw's frown deepened and he shook his head heavily. 'I wouldn't recommend that, Tanner. The people in this town remember you and they don't like you. It could cause more trouble for you

– and for me. Why don't you just saddle your pony and get out of my town before I'm forced to put you in jail under protective custody?'

'You wouldn't. . . .' John Tanner began, but he knew by the expression on the marshal's face and from past experience that McGraw would do just that if provoked. 'I guess I'll be leaving soon, McGraw.'

'I guess you will,' the lawman said. Then he turned and stomped heavily on his way, leaving Tanner in a predicament. He could not have ridden all this way on the trail of the kidnappers only to give it up now. But getting himself locked up in the jail would be even less productive. Maybe if he waited until nightfall and made a few inquiries. . . .

Then he saw a familiar face. The sallow, blond-haired man, Wes Dalton. One of the kidnappers, or so Ben Canasta thought, Dalton having left the C-bar-C on the morning after the robbery. Wes Dalton was standing in the doorway of the stable opposite the one where Tanner had put up his gray horse.

He started that way.

John Tanner's movements were clumsy – his taped ribs allowed little natural movement. But he was determined and angry as he strode that way. Wes Dalton didn't recognize Tanner until he was three strides away from him. They did not know each

49

other well, and Tanner's face was shadowed by the wide brim of his Stetson hat. Suddenly Dalton did recognize him and he voiced a little squeak, his hand lowering toward his holstered gun.

It was too late. Tanner already had his Colt drawn and in two more paces he had it leveled at Wes Dalton's belly and was nudging him back into the shadowed interior of the stable.

'What do you want?' Dalton asked, his hands held high as Tanner took the robber's gun and hurled it away.

'You guess,' Tanner said in a nasty voice. 'Where's Becky Canasta?' he demanded, glancing around to make sure no other kidnapper was slipping up on him.

'How would I know?' Wes Dalton said with force although his voice quavered. 'Not with me, that's for sure!'

'What do you mean?' Tanner demanded. 'Tell me all about it – your life might depend on it,' he added as he steadied his cocked revolver and leveled it at Dalton's mid-section. Fear caused Wes Dalton's face to tighten. Now his hands were shaking slightly as he continued to hold them high.

'Listen, Tanner, it's like this – we rode out to Split Rock and we all went our own ways. I figured to ride into Knox and spend some money, have a good time. Morgan and Charlie Cox took the other trails. You know, toward Ruidoso and Las Palmas.'

'Which one took which road?'

'I don't know. I was first to leave,' Dalton said. 'I knew I could make Knox that night and sleep in a bed. Morgan Pride and Charlie figured their horses would need some rest before striking out on the long trail. They decided to sleep out at Split Rock.'

'Who has the girl?' Tanner asked savagely.

'It must be Morgan Pride, but I couldn't swear to it. All I know is we all decided to split up, make it harder to follow us.'

Internally Tanner sighed, though he continued to show Dalton his wolfish expression. That was it – if Dalton was telling the truth, Tanner had wasted three days and nights in Knox, taking a brutal beating for his trouble while Morgan Pride and Charlie Cox had ridden a lot of miles away on the long desert.

Worse, Ted Everly and his men had had a lot of time to reach Knox as well and were probably even now in town, waiting for Tanner to emerge. They would have checked the stables and seen that his gray horse was still here.

John hated to admit it, but Marshal McGraw was right – it was time to leave the town of Knox.

'Can I put my hands down, Tanner? I told you

everything you wanted to know.'

'Go ahead,' John said with resignation. 'There's just one more little thing – I want your cut of the money you stole from Ben Canasta.'

'But that will leave me. . . .' Wes Dalton sputtered. Tanner had no pity to spare.

'It will leave you no worse off than you were before. No worse off than Ben Canasta is now. You boys should have stayed around to get your pay. It would have been only another few days.'

'We knew you were coming back,' Dalton said dismally. 'Morgan saw the letter you wrote to Ben Canasta.'

'You could have had a comfortable life on the C-bar-C,' Tanner told him. 'Now you have nothing. Well, it's your own greedy fault! I'll take that money now.'

FOUR

John Tanner trailed out of Knox at mid-morning as the color had faded from the eastern sky and the silver sun began to heat the long desert before him. The main street of the tiny town was nearly deserted, still he kept his eyes open for familiar faces. From what Wes Dalton had told him – if he was to be believed – Charlie Cox and Morgan Pride were either in Las Palmas or Ruidoso. There was no choice but to look there as well, although both had had time to reach those towns, rest and purchase whatever supplies they needed and head farther toward the horizon. John Tanner had decided upon Las Palmas first simply because it was nearer. His ribs were already bothering him after only a few minutes in the saddle.

He saw no one he recognized as he left Knox behind him.

But there had been that one moment when he had glimpsed a small figure at the curtained window of the hat shop, looking out at him as he passed. That had caused John a small pang of regret, but what was a man to do? He had his obligations to attend to.

He turned the gray southward, away from the direct glare of the sun and plodded on through the long day toward Las Palmas. Every step of the horse jolted his ribcage and after a while his battered skull developed a throbbing headache. He would have abandoned the gray and taken a coach to Las Palmas, except the stable man had advised him that there was no connection between Knox and Las Palmas these days. It was doubtful that he would have been more comfortable on a jolting stage-coach anyway.

Far away he could still see the forested hills that rose above C-bar-C land, but on his route the land was flat red-sand desert once more. By noon his horse was wearing down and the high sun felt hot enough to raise blisters on his back. Still he saw no shade.

He had ridden this way many years ago, but time had erased his memory of the land. It seemed to

Tanner that he and Joe Block had nooned through the heat of the day near a rill. But Joe had been the older, more experienced man, and Tanner had followed him without taking real notice of the trail they followed. He only recalled the silver-bright stream and a clutter of willow brush along its banks. He wished now that he had been more attentive.

John wanted to swing down from the saddle and rest even if he had to use his horse for shade. The trouble was he was not so certain that he could climb back aboard once he got down, and such an experiment would surely do nothing to aid his horse which was also suffering in the heat.

They ambled on, the horse's hoofs whispering in the dry sand, occasionally chinking when the animal happened to strike a steel shoe against a rock. John tried not to doze, did, and awoke in the saddle, scolding himself bitterly. The last thing he need to do was fall from the saddle with his horse possibly continuing on without him.

It was not until mid-afternoon that Tanner saw the gray horse lift its head and snuffle loudly. It had sensed something. Tanner looked ahead and then slowly his desert-blinded eyes were able to pick out a long low line of gray-green a half a mile or so ahead. That could be the stream, almost certainly was. Vegetation did not flourish in this country without some source of water, not even willows which had the ability to go dormant through dry spells. He urged the weary horse onward, knowing that it could be hopeful imagining. The roots of the willows might have found an underwater source, but would there be any surface water along the course of the rill?

With incredible relief, Tanner found the edge of the water-cut channel and looking down, saw the mirror sheen of a pond in the sunlight. The stream was not flowing, but that was unimportant. There was enough water in the small pond to serve his needs. He started the now-eager horse down the sandy bank, searching for a path through the densely growing willows.

After two false starts, he managed to work his way to where the pond lay. Looking to his left he could see that the rill was indeed still running, if you could count that pencil-thin trickle of water moving along the bottom of the gully a stream. No matter – the pond was there. Approaching it, Tanner startled a three-point mule deer which bounded away into the security of the thicket, leaving the pond to Tanner and his horse.

He rode his gray to the very edge of the pond and let it lower its head into the water. Tanner was still reluctant to swing down, afraid of not being able to remount. With its thirst assuaged, knowing the source of water now, the gray would be less likely to wander off, leaving Tanner alone on the desert. He sat waiting patiently while the horse drank its fill before slowly, with infinite care he swung out of leather. The motion sent waves of pain flaring across his ribs. By the time he got both feet on the ground he had to lean against the horse.

He thought grimly that he could still be resting in Candice Moore's big pink bed – but where would that leave Becky Canasta? Another day or two farther along the lost trail. And Ben Canasta? It would put him a day or two closer to a desperate death.

Tanner staggered to the pond and dropped to hands and knees, drinking deeply like an animal. When he managed to rise again, his head was throbbing, his breath short, his legs trembling. He was riding himself to death. There were some willows tall enough to offer shade from the heat of day and, gathering up the gray's reins, he started that way across the white river sand toward the copse.

John decided that the horse had to be unsaddled and after unfastening the cinches he eyed the saddle which seemed immovable in his present condition. He gripped its cantle and pommel and tried to swing it to the ground, but he collapsed to one knee in the sand. It was just too much for him. Well, he reflected, that morning he had not even been able to put on his own shirt – what had he expected? The stable man had saddled for him back in Knox; John Tanner had started out under the happy illusion that his strength would soon return even though the long desert trail was bound to contribute to further debilitation. Mind over matter had not worked. He had been a plain fool to start out feeling as he did.

Stubbornly he rose and gripped the saddle again. A voice called out from behind him:

'Hold it, partner.'

Tanner turned, expecting to find a man pointing a gun at him.

'Who. . . ?' John wanted to know, for he did not recognize the young blue-eyed man with the cheerful smile who approached him from out of the copse.

'Name's Chad Garret,' the man said. 'Just hold on there for a second. I've been watching you. Want me to unsaddle for you?'

'If you could. . . .' Tanner said, feeling grateful, mistrustful, and ashamed of his condition all at once.

'Sure thing,' the tall, younger man said, coming toward the horse. 'I've been banged up a few times myself. Are you shot?'

'No – it's my ribs,' Tanner said as Chad Garret swung the saddle easily to the ground, swept the blanket from the gray's back and tossed it on top of the saddle.

'Better come over to the trees and rest awhile,' Chad said, 'it looks like you've had a long ride. I've got some coffee boiled; it won't take but a minute to heat it up again.'

As Tanner sagged to the sandy ground beneath the willows, he watched silently as Chad Garret restarted a tiny fire he had built. Finally he asked Garret:

'What are you doing way out here?'

'Me?' Garret said with a quick laugh. He stood, dusting his hands on his faded jeans. He tilted his hat back from his forehead and told Tanner. 'I'm just sort of roaming the desert, you might say. I'm not moving far or fast – I travel a few hours at dawn, wait the heat of the day out and travel on a few miles about sundown. No destination in mind.'

'I see,' Tanner said, liking the smiling young man. Now Chad Garret brought Tanner a cup of dark, warm coffee and handed it to him.

'My coffee's close to tar,' Garret said, seating himself on an Indian blanket he had spread out on the sand. 'Sorry, it's the best I have to offer.'

'It's all right,' Tanner said, sipping it gratefully,

although Chad Garret was close to right in his description of the brew. Tanner picked a few coffee grounds which had not dropped to the bottom of the pot from his tongue and inquired. 'Have you seen anybody else out here.'

'Not for two days,' Garret said. 'Then it was a party of Indians. I let them go their way, they let me go mine. They didn't look hostile, but you never can tell.'

'No,' Tanner agreed. You never can judge anyone by looks alone. Chad Garret, for example – he gave the impression of being a man who might be on the run from something. That did not matter at the moment. It was not John Tanner's business, and the young, smiling man had helped him out.

'Where are you heading?' Garret asked. A tarantula had passed his blanket and he was idly tormenting the wooly insect with a twig.

'Las Palmas. I was hoping to make it sometime tomorrow. You don't happen to know how far off it is, do you?'

'No, not really. I've heard of the place, but I've never seen it,' Garret answered, letting the tarantula continue on its way, tossing the twig into the dying fire. He stretched out on his back, his hat shading his eyes from the sunlight falling through tangle of willow brush overhead. 'If you want some advice, though, I'd recommend that you do what I do – travel in the cool of morning and close to sundown. Get what rest you can in between. You might think you're losing a lot of time that way, but it beats having your horse die on you out on the flats – or losing your own life. Besides, partner, I don't think you're in any kind of shape for a long ride.'

All of that was true enough. John Tanner was eager to reach trail's end, to find Becky, but he would be of little use to her if he ended up only as buzzard feed. He closed his eyes and tried to sleep through the heat of the lonesome day.

When he awoke again it was to something nudging his shoulder. He reached automatically for his Colt, but saw that it was only Chad Garret hovering over him, a grin on his face. There was already some color in the western skies as the sun sank lower.

'Time to get going,' Garret said. He did not attempt to help Tanner up, having no idea what might cause John more pain.

Corkscrewing to his feet, John found that he felt better than he had expected, certainly better than he had that morning. He still had a headache, but it was of the dull sort. His ribs ached but were not filled with fiery pain. The water and the rest had done him some good. Chad Garret had led his pinto pony out of concealment and had saddled it. Now he prepared Tanner's gray for riding.

'I was thinking,' Garret said as Tanner approached, 'I might just as well ride along with you – if you have no objections.'

'None,' Tanner said after a brief hesitation. After all, he still did not know this man, but it was obvious that he could use a saddle partner. It was a minor humiliation – Tanner had always thought of himself as a man able to take care of himself. Yet how much help had he needed lately? Too much. A man in Knox to saddle his horse, a man out here to saddle it again. . . . A woman to feed him, bathe him, dress him.

He refused to think any more about Candice Moore. She had gone back to her old way of life by now, and he to his. Carefully he swung aboard his horse, surprised and pleased to find that it was much easier on this night. Maybe he was healing fast, if not as quickly as he might have hoped.

Mounted now, the two men crossed the sandy creekbed and emerged on to the long desert once again. The cheerful Chad Garret was singing as they rode:

Farewell, señorita
I now must be going. . . .

The miles passed easily as the purple light of dusk darkened the land and the stars blinked on one by one above the long desert. The horses, watered and well-rested, moved easily beneath them. John Tanner found himself in a better mood than he had for a long while. In the far distance Tanner saw, or thought he did, the flickering of lights, which in that direction could only be from the town of Las Palmas.

'Looks like we could make it there in an hour or so,' Chad said, looking in the direction of the lights, 'if you're feeling up to it.'

'I'd like to try,' Tanner answered. 'The horses need rest and with luck we could find us a place to sleep where there are no scorpions. Maybe even a hotel with real beds. I believe that would help my ribs.'

'I guess it would,' Chad Garret agreed. 'But there's one thing I haven't admitted to, John: I haven't a nickel in my jeans.'

'I'll take care of it,' John offered. He had Wes Dalton's share of the stolen money in his saddle-bags. Ben Canasta certainly wouldn't begrudge him spending a few dollars on a decent meal and a hotel room.

'You never did tell me how you happened to find yourself out here, in this condition,' Chad Garret said as they rode steadily toward Las Palmas.

John did so now, telling most of what had occurred down his backtrail. Chad listened thoughtfully. 'So you're hoping to find the girl in Las Palmas.'

'Becky and probably Morgan Pride – he must be the one she rode off with, the man who planned this all.'

'I hope it works out for you – and for the old man,' Chad said. 'I had a grandfather who owned a ranch up in Colorado. He kept getting weaker from simple age. As he got sicker, the men around him, people he trusted, starting culling beef from his herd, figuring the old man would never rise again to ride out on the range and check his cattle.'

'What happened?'

'He got well, tracked down two of the rustlers and shot them dead,' Chad said without smiling.

John nodded thoughtfully. Ahead now they could see the shapes of the town's structures. He was not even definitely sure that this was Las Palmas, but it was the only town of any size in the area. As they approached they spotted a cluster of five palm trees standing on the edge of a streambed, presumably the trees from which the village had taken its name.

'This must be it,' Chad commented.

'Seems like it.'

'What do you mean to do first?'

'Much as I'd like to start hunting right now, it's late and I think we need rest and food first. Morning's soon enough.' Assuming that Morgan Pride was even in town – the kidnapper had three days lead on John. And what about Becky? Where would she be? Held captive, or was she a willing accomplice as Monique had asserted, spending her days in a hotel, dining well? There was no guessing. John Tanner didn't want to believe that the girl had betrayed her father. There was only one way to find out the truth – that meant finding Becky, listening to her story.

The main street of Las Palmas was rutted and here and there sprouted weeds and stands of creosote. The face of one building was brightly illuminated – a saloon, no doubt – but the rest of the town was dark, sleeping in this desert night. They found a stable with no trouble and an indifferent balding man in overalls led their horses in.

Chad said: 'Can you unsaddle the gray for us. I'll take care of my own pony.'

Sliding to the ground with less pain that he had had that morning, but with more stiffness, Tanner watched as Chad Garret unsaddled his pinto pony, swinging the saddle with ease on to a stall partition. The seemingly uncaring stablehand unsaddled the gray and slipped its bit, hanging the bridle on a nail in the wall. Tanner fished a five-dollar gold piece from his pocket.

'Make sure they get a bait of oats each, won't you?' he said, slipping the coin on to the callused palm of the stableman. 'They've had a hard ride.'

The morose stablehand only nodded mutely. Tanner wanted to question the man about Becky, but he doubted he would get much out of him. Maybe in the morning.

They both trusted their saddles to the man in the stable and walked across the rutted road toward the false-fronted building which advertised itself with a sign dangling from its awning: 'Hotel.'

Opening the door to the narrow lobby, they could smell steak searing somewhere in an adjacent dining hall. 'Better and better,' Chad Garret said. 'That is . . . if you're springing for dinner as well.'

'I am; let's make sure they have a room first.'

'I'm starting to be awful glad that I ran into you out there,' Chad said with a wide grin. 'Food's a little hard to come by on the desert. I went two days eating only rattlesnake meat.'

'We'll get you fed,' John Tanner said, realizing that he was equally lucky to have come across Chad Garret. Without Chad's help he might not have even made it to Las Palmas.

With a room key in their hands, they were passed on through to the diner. The ceiling was low; it was still warm inside. A few travelers and a couple of rough-dressed cowhands from some local ranch sat scattered across the room which had individual tables covered with red-checked cloths and not your usual plank on barrels.

A nice-looking young blonde waitress motioned them to a table in the corner and they seated themselves while she scribbled down an order from another table: a man who was dressed like a drummer sat hand on chin, talking to a girl in a scarlet dress, apparently a local saloon girl enjoying a free steak dinner.

'Love!' Chad said with a smile, nodding toward the couple.

'A man has to pretend he's found it now and then, even if it's only for a night, until the next coach pulls out.'

The waitress, a little older than Tanner had first guessed, came to their table. Now they could see the perspiration stains at her armpits, the weariness in her eyes.

'What'll it be, gents?'

'What's everyone else having?' Chad asked.

'I can have steaks fried for you, beans and corn on the cob.'

'Two plates of each,' John Tanner replied immediately. 'I can't think of anything that sounds better.'

'How do you want your steaks?'

'Burn 'em,' Chad said before John could answer. As the waitress walked away toward the kitchen, Chad said, 'That way, they can never get your order wrong.'

It was very late before they had finished eating. Only the drummer and the dancehall girl still lingered in the restaurant. The drummer was obviously trying to proposition her, and she was playing at being coy, trying to measure how much she could take the mark for.

They walked back into the hotel. No one was behind the counter. Their room was at the rear of the building, obviously not the best they had to offer, but what did that matter to two desert rats? Their stomachs were full; they had a roof over their heads. Chad lit the lantern on the table and started undressing. Tanner started to take his shirt off, then changed his mind as he raised his arms and fresh pain shot through his ribs. It seemed like a daunting task to reach down and pull his boots off and so he simply lay back on the sagging bed and fell almost immediately to sleep.

For now he had satisfied his hunger, found a soft

place to lie down; sometimes that is all that is required for comfort.

The war could wait until tomorrow.

FIVE

The night settled into cool darkness. John Tanner slept only briefly and then awoke to find someone prowling the room. It was only Chad Garret, of course. Tanner had nearly forgotten about hooking up with Chad. Now the young man stood at the window, staring out meditatively at the night.

'What is it, Chad?'

'I've got a troubling feeling,' Chad answered. 'Do you have ten dollars you can let me have?'

'I suppose so,' Tanner answered, sitting up on the edge of his bed. 'You're not pulling out on me, are you, Chad?'

'No. There's something I should take care of.'

Tanner managed to dig up ten silver dollars, and

handed them over to Chad, not asking him what he wanted the money for. Chad had given him ten dollars worth of service, no matter what he was up to.

Tugging on his boots, Chad went to the doorway and said to John Tanner, 'Don't go back to sleep until you see me again.'

That was a little mysterious, but John agreed. He rose stiffly from the bed and stood at the window himself, looking out at the dark desert town. There were only a few scattered lights – not counting the saloon which was still going great guns.

John heard boot steps approaching the room and he turned, automatically reaching for his holstered gun. It was only Garret. He came in wearing a satisfied look. 'Collect your gear, John,' Chad said.

'What are we playing at?' Tanner asked warily.

'We're changing rooms. Remember we wrote our names in the hotel register. Thinking about that for some time, I decided I didn't like the idea of someone who might be waiting for you wandering in and finding your room number written down. The night clerk didn't mind, or at least he was susceptible to a little bribery.' Chad held up another room key.

'I asked him not to write the change down and he

agreed. So – gather your things, we're moving next door.'

'Sounds smart to me,' Tanner said. Thinking about it later as he stretched out on his new bed, Chad's move seemed a little slick for someone who had not been on the run before. It was difficult to think of the affable Chad Garret as an outlaw, a man on the run. But he seemed to have some experience with these matters. Mentally John shrugged. It did no good to ponder on the possibilities too deeply, besides Chad's notion did furnish another layer of protection for him. Because if Morgan Pride was still in town, he would be watching his back trail, suspecting that someone might have followed him this far.

Las Palmas slept; John Tanner slept. There was a cool breeze drifting into the room from off the desert, carrying the scent of sage. It was nearly three a.m. when a crashing sound woke them up. Chad was up from his bed in a hurry. With an uncomfortable groan, John Tanner rolled from his own bed and reached for his holstered gun belt.

'Where did that come from?' John asked.

'Next door!' Chad whispered back. 'Someone booted the door open.'

'Morgan Pride?'

'I wouldn't know – let's find out.'

Creeping along the hallway wall to the adjacent room, they heard two men growling and grumbling to each other as they searched the empty room. John let Chad go in first. He followed with his pistol in hand. From the doorway, Tanner saw one of the men rush at Chad, his fists wildly flailing. Chad kicked the attacker in the knee and as he doubled up with pain, Chad brought his knee up into the man's face. The thug's head snapped back, and his eyes rolled up in his skull. Chad let the man topple face first to the floor.

Beyond Chad Garret, Tanner saw a man he recognized, turning toward Chad, his revolver in his hand.

'Hold it right there, Charlie!' Tanner commanded, displaying his own Colt. 'Drop that pistol right now or I'll give it to you.'

'You?' Charlie said dumbly as he opened his hand and let his handgun clatter to the floor boards.

'Back away with your hands up,' Tanner said.

'You know this man?' Chad Garret asked.

'Charlie Cox. He's one of the robbers, one of the kidnappers.' Charlie watched mutely, eyeing John Tanner, glancing at his own weapon lying on the floor between them. His pistol was too far away, Tanner too near to consider trying anything. Charlie stood trembling with fury.

'Where's Morgan Pride?' Tanner demanded.

'How would I know?' Charlie Cox asked truculently.

'Wes Dalton told me that he was either here or in Ruidoso.'

'You found Wes?'

'I did, up in Knox. I didn't want to kill him, but he wouldn't tell me everything I wanted to know,' John Tanner lied.

'Now wait a minute,' Charlie Cox said, appearing nervous now. 'No need for this – I'll tell you where Morgan is.'

'Fine. Down in Ruidoso?'

'Unless he decided to move on.' He was speaking with more confidence now.

'He has Becky with him?'

'As far as I know,' Cox answered sullenly.

'What do you think?' Tanner said, glancing at Chad. 'Should we take him out on the desert and leave him for the coyotes?'

Chad shrugged and said expressionlessly, 'It makes no difference to me. If they find his body in this room it might throw suspicion on us. We don't need that.'

'Now wait a minute!' Charlie Cox said, his nervousness returning. 'I've answered all your questions.'

'Not quite,' Tanner said. There's more I need to know. Where's your cut from the robbery, Charlie?'

'What? No! I'm damned if I will.'

Tanner glanced again at Chad Garret and asked, 'Isn't that the same thing Wes Dalton said?'

'Almost his exact words before we. . . .'

'I'll tell you, damnit!' Charlie Cox said as Chad drew his own pistol and cocked the hammer.

'The money's no good to you now, anyway,' Tanner told the cowering thief. 'Either we kill you – which is most likely – or we turn you into the law. Do it our way and you'll stay alive and out of prison. Do it your way and you're taking a big chance, Charlie.'

'Damn you!' Charlie said in a hoarse voice. A last bit of bravado. His forehead was beaded perspiration, his raised hands trembled. 'I'll hand over the money.'

After recovering the money from its hiding place in Charlie Cox's room, Tanner and Chad backed out and hurried off. There was no telling – Cox might have had another gun in his room.

It was far too early, but they decided to travel on before Cox could get his nerve up again, possibly summoning some help.

The stable hand emerged from some back room hide-away, his eyes as red as radishes, and with small displays of ill-temper brought their horses out and saddled the gray for Tanner. John softened the man's anger a little with a two-dollar tip and the two men walked their horses out into the cool desert night, swung aboard and rode out on to the star-bright desert.

'I wish the man would have waited until after breakfast,' Chad Garret said as they headed south in the direction of Ruidoso.

'You hungry again?'

'Still. Two days on rattlesnake meat can do that to you.'

'I'll see that your stomach is filled in Ruidoso,' John promised. They rode silently for a while across the flat desert. Once Chad chuckled, and Tanner asked him what was funny.

'The bluff you ran back there with that Charlie Cox – threatening to take him out on the desert and leave his body there. That really shook him.'

'Who says I was bluffing?' Tanner answered quietly. 'I didn't know you could fight like that,' he said to a thoughtful Chad Garret.

'Well, I knew you couldn't – that's why I went in first. I figured we were in for some kind of trouble.'

'It worked out well enough, that's all that matters.'

After another quarter of a mile Chad asked, 'Did you recover all of the money?'

'Most of it, I guess. He's sure to have spent some, and we didn't make him empty out his pockets.'

'Well, the old man will be happy to get most of it back,' Chad said, after guiding his pinto into and out of a dry wash.

'I suppose so,' Tanner answered, wondering if Ben Canasta would be alive when he got back to the C-bar-C, the shape he was in. Wondering if the money would even matter to Ben if Tanner returned to the ranch without Becky.

They rode on resolutely through the night, both to put some distance between themselves and Charlie Cox who knew where they were heading, and because Tanner needed to find Becky Canasta. Despite the hazards of the night ride, when the sky began to color faintly in the east, they found themselves able to make out the pre-dawn gray shapes of the buildings of Ruidoso, and by the time the faint colors in the eastern sky flared up with violent reds and deep orange, they were walking their horses down the deserted main street of the border town.

Was Morgan Pride still here, or had he decided by now to ride for the border? John would find out, some way this morning. He had been long on the trail, and decided then and there that he would waste no more time in his search. He would have liked to eat, to sleep, but he already knew he would not. He would track down Morgan Pride, find out where Becky was. Then perhaps there would be time to rest.

They took their horses to the nearest livery stable and left them in the hands of a young, simple-looking young man with blank eyes. Tanner offered to pay, but the kid said:

'I can't count money. You'll have to pay when the boss is here.'

They left instructions on how they wanted the weary horses cared for and went out into the brilliant sunshine of the cool morning. No clouds stained the sky. It was going to be another hot day. When was it not? Tanner had not felt a breath of cool air since riding down from the mountains on to C-bar-C land.

That seemed like so long ago.

'There's a restaurant open,' Chad Garret said. 'Somewhere. I can smell coffee and frying ham.'

'Let's find it,' Tanner said, 'and I'll set you up.'

'You're not going to eat?' Chad asked with surprise. Tanner shook his head negatively. Chad said, 'Look, John, maybe it's not my business, but you aren't going to get much detective work done at this time of the morning. And if the man has already left town, you'll have another long ride ahead of you. You don't want to do that on an empty stomach.'

Tanner had to agree with the logic of that although his conscience, his need to finally find the end of the trail, drove him on. His stomach growled in disagreement as they discovered the restaurant.

'I suppose you're right,' John agreed reluctantly, and so they stepped on through the restaurant door, Tanner carrying his heavy saddle-bags over his shoulder. They treated themselves to coffee – a lot of it – biscuits, ham and even eggs, probably purchased from some local farm wife trying to earn a few extra dollars.

The meal was eaten mostly in silence except for Chad's comments on the few good-looking women in the establishment. They had talked the past to death along the trail, and they knew nothing of the future.

John had noticed in the livery barn that swinging down from his horse was much easier this morning. Tentatively he had stretched his arms overhead and the pain which had been his constant companion since Knox was dulled appreciably. He seemed finally to be healing despite the rough usage his body had taken.

Standing on the sunlit porch in front of the restaurant after breakfast, John Tanner felt pleased with himself. Stomach full, much of the stolen money recovered, and Morgan Pride and Becky, as newcomers in town were sure to have been seen and noticed. Even if they had left Ruidoso someone would have seen them as they traveled on. He was so close, and his eagerness was a swelling desire in his heart. He wanted to end it now.

'There's a hotel right across the street,' Chad Garret pointed out.

'I couldn't sleep,' John Tanner said. 'You feel free to take a nap.'

'I think I have to, John,' Chad said. 'I think you'd be wise to do the same.'

'I have to keep going,' John said as they crossed to the hotel, pausing to let a huge ore wagon pass. 'They're here somewhere. I have to find her.'

At the hotel entrance, Chad said, 'You make me feel that I'm letting you down, John. Do you want me to go along?'

'No. You've done enough for me, Chad. This I can do on my own.'

'All right – if you have no luck, or if you have luck, come and find me.'

The male clerk behind the counter looked pouched and weary as if he had had no sleep either. Tanner asked about Morgan Pride as Chad registered, but got only a negative shake of the head for an answer.

'Are there other hotels in this town?' John inquired.

'Two, but they're hardly up to our standards,' the clerk snapped.

'Just asking,' John said, paying for the room which had two beds and was upstairs. John memorized the room number and then walked Chad to the foot of the stairs. 'You'd better take this and shove it under my bed,' John said, taking the saddlebags from his shoulder. 'They'll just slow me down, and I wouldn't want anyone to find me carrying that much money around.'

'All right,' Chad agreed. 'I'll keep one eye open, just in case. Though I can't see any thieves taking me for a mark, looking like I do.'

Tanner agreed. Both men were trail-dusty, wearing ragged shirts and faded jeans, hardly the sort thieves would be eyeing for a score.

'Just lock the door behind you,' John advised. 'We can't be too careful.'

'And you, John,' Chad said seriously, 'you be careful too. This Morgan Pride sounds like a dangerous man – and there's no certainty that Charlie Cox didn't decide to follow us down here. He knows where we were going.'

That was true. It was also true that John had no idea where Ted Everly and whoever was riding with him had gone. John had been assuming that Everly had given up and turned back by now. You never knew. Maybe he was spurred on by Monique's hatred of John Tanner, his promise to her to get the murderer of Matt Doyle.

There was no point in thinking about all of that right now. He had to first find Morgan Pride and Becky. He had made a promise to a dying man that he would do so.

The morning was spent strolling the boardwalks of Ruidoso – what there were of them, sometimes stopping to talk to shopkeepers, idlers, asking casually if they had seen someone resembling either Becky or Morgan Pride. He told many tales about his reason for asking about them. The stories varied, but the answers to his questions were always they same. No one had seen them.

The responses at the two hotels produced the same results. *Where, then, were they?*

The answer, if it was that, came to him near midday with the silver sun shimmering down through a white sky.

Morgan Pride had sacks of money. He did not wish to be seen. How long did he wish to remain in Ruidoso? Maybe weeks, months until he was certain his back trail was clear. John rose wearily from the wooden bench in front of a saddlery and made his way toward a real estate agent's office.

'That's not the name he gave me,' the young, spectacled man he talked to told John. 'But, yes, they were here. His wife was quite pretty. I couldn't help noticing that, but she seemed extremely upset or nervous as her husband took the property. It's a small cabin over on Wolf Creek. The man said he wanted to be sure his wife liked living out there first, so I agreed to rent it to him for a few months with an option to buy. He paid cash for the lease and they went on their way.'

'What name did he give you?' John asked.

'Is there something wrong?' the real estate agent asked uneasily.

'No. What name?'

'Colquist. Arthur Colquist.'

After the realtor had sketched a rough map so that John Tanner could find the Wolf Creek property, Tanner went back out into the brilliant glare of sunlight, crossed to the stable once again and led his sleepy horse out of its stall. Chad Garret's pinto horse in the next stall opened one eye as they moved past it. John considered asking Chad to come along, but the man was undoubtedly deep in a well-earned sleep. Besides, John wished to finish this by himself. It was he who had taken on the job, not Chad.

'Want me to saddle your horse?' the stable man asked.

'No. I can do it myself,' John said with a kind of perverse pride. He removed his saddle from the partition and swung it up and on to the gray's back. The movement hurt him – not with the kind of saber-like shock he might have suffered a few days ago, but still it caused a spasm of pain.

John wondered if he were healing, or if the pain had been such a constant that he was simply learning to endure it.

Early afternoon found him riding out on to the desert once more. Taking his bearings from the rough map, he followed a gully through a stand of cottonwood trees, their leaves silver in the sunlight. The gully, he decided, must have been Wolf Creek – a seasonal stream.

Pointing the horse's nose toward a distant knobby hill, John rode on. The real estate agent had estimated the distance from town to be about three miles. It was much farther than that. It seemed that Morgan Pride had chosen the most remote hideout possible.

Finally John saw what he had been looking for. From the crest of a sandy knoll, he could see the two weather-grayed wooden buildings below. A small house, a tiny barn. He let his horse blow as he tried to formulate a plan. There seemed to be no way to creep up to the house unseen. The creosote-studded desert was flat ground for hundreds of yards around the house. Were they even in the house? John had to believe that they were. Why go to all of the trouble of renting the house when all Pride wanted to do was rest for a few days, then, perhaps striking out toward the Mexican border?

Warily, John started his horse down the rocky face of the knoll, the sun now on his back as it lowered toward the western horizon. He heard a sound from the tiny barn – a horse nickered. They were still there then – or someone was.

Having achieved the flats, John approached the house from the blind side. There were two small windows in front, none he could see anywhere else, unless there was a back window he could not see from this angle.

He checked the loads in his Colt unnecessarily. It was always loaded. It was only a nervous gesture.

He pulled up the gray beside the stable where he could not be seen from the house. And if his horse were to be heard to nicker it would be assumed that it was one of their own horses – for passing the barn door, Morgan could see that there were two horses stabled up within its dark, musty interior. Palming his Colt, he slipped up to the side of the house. It took him a minute to gather his courage. Without a plan, he was risking much, but this was the job he had accepted, and this would be his last day on the job.

One way or the other.

There was a narrow porch in front of the house, but John was reluctant to use it. It was very old and likely swayed and creaked when someone passed over it. Instead he made his way directly to the front door and after three deep breaths leaped across the sagging steps there, putting his shoulder to the door which burst open, slamming against the wall. He didn't have to wait long to find Morgan Pride.

The robber was sitting at a wooden table, his back to John Tanner who had his gun cocked and ready to fire.

'Wes?' Morgan asked glancing toward the sun-bright rectangle of the door, blinking into the glare of the desert sun.

'Wes won't be coming,' John told Pride. 'Neither will Charlie Cox.'

Morgan Pride remained motionless while his eyes adjusted to the harsh light of the day. He abruptly half-rose, shouting out, 'John Tanner!'

'That's right. I wouldn't try it, Morgan. I've got you in my sights. There's no way you're going to beat me.'

'Listen, Tanner,' Morgan Pride said, hoisting his hands high as he rose cautiously from the table. 'You know I never. . . .'

Pride was snake-quick. Tanner should have just shot the man in cold blood as he sat at the table, for Pride drew his pistol and rolled to the floor, firing three hasty shots at John before he rose to one knee to try sending a more carefully aimed bullet in John's direction.

Deliberately then, Tanner shot the man once, twice and Morgan Pride jerked spastically, trying to come to his feet. His arms flailed; his right knee buckled beneath him and his revolver dropped from his fingers.

'That was damned stupid,' Tanner said to the dying man. But Morgan Pride had always had more heart than common sense. Reflecting, Tanner decided that this was the only way it could have ended – with one of them dead. What was he to do? Escort Pride back to the C-bar-C with Pride watching every minute, waiting for the first opportunity to break free, watching Tanner as he slept, looking for a moment's inattention?

He stood over the unmoving Morgan Pride for a time, studying the dead man's contorted features. Then he heard a small sound from the other room, and cocking his pistol, Tanner started that way, wondering if he had guessed wrong about Pride being alone out here.

She leaned against the far wall, facing it. Becky's hands were clenched into fists. She looked around fearfully, then recognized Tanner and rushed to him, her eyes filled with tears. 'I knew you would come, John,' she said. 'It's been a nightmare! Did you . . . kill him?'

'He won't bother you again.'

'I had to do whatever he said,' Becky said with a trembling lip. 'I even had to pretend to like him. Otherwise . . . he said that all I was doing was slowing him down.'

Tanner nodded without replying. Was he listening to the truth or to a hurriedly concocted story? The real estate agent had said that she appeared fearful – that was the only evidence he had that Becky Canasta had been accompanying Morgan Pride as a hostage. He had deep reservations, but as he looked into her damp blue eyes, saw the fear there, he almost believed her; wanted to believe her. Perhaps he could find out something definite on the trail home. Ben Canasta wanted his daughter back, and Tanner meant to deliver her. He got on with more practical matters.

'Change into riding clothes and get your horse ready to trail out of here, Becky. I'm taking you back to the C-bar-C. Untether Pride's horse and let it follow along with us or stay out here, whichever it chooses to do. There's only one other thing:

'Where is the money hidden?'

SIX

'Praise the Lord,' Tanner, who was not an especially religious man, breathed as they reached the town limits of Ruidoso late that afternoon. Becky Canasta, dirt on her face, her expression glum, hair straggling free of her straw hat, bore little resemblance to the goddess he had once seen in the moonlight. She had a small travelling bag tied to her saddlehorn. Just now she was wearing blue jeans, and a red plaid shirt.

She looked far more exhausted than Tanner felt. But after all she was returning from a life of peril and entering an uncertain new life.

As for Tanner – now it was done. He had the money stolen from Ben Canasta, minus that spent by the Morgan Pride gang along the way, and he had Becky. He was looking forward to returning to the C-bar-C, having done his job well. For now he meant to take a much-needed rest. Knowing the way, Tanner rode directly to the hotel, still feeling the warm glow of success.

'I need a bath, a bed,' Becky said in a dry, throttled voice.

'Any minute now,' Tanner said as he swung down from his horse, shouldered the saddle-bags which contained Morgan Pride's share of the stolen money. Becky had hesitated when Tanner had demanded the money, but finally she had showed him a disused pantry where Pride had concealed the loot.

Now as they entered the hotel, the weight of the saddle-bags on his shoulder was reassuring rather than being a burden. They passed the desk of the hotel, and Becky inquired with her eyes. 'I've already got a room here,' Tanner explained. 'We'll get you another after I've had the time to sit down with Chad Garret and talk things through.'

Becky's eyes were dubious but not necessarily worried. After all she had spent the past week in the company of a gunman. Walking into Tanner's room, despite the fact that it was something a lady just did not do, held little threat for her.

Tanner stopped in front of the hotel room door, rapped twice, frowned as he got no answer, then

figured that Chad was already up and gone, probably to some restaurant to alleviate his constant
hunger.

'Just a minute,' Tanner said, and he stepped into
the room. It was empty; Chad had gone out somewhere. Gesturing Becky in, he dropped his
saddle-bags on the unused bed and heard Becky
drop her travelling bag on the floor behind him.
The room was musty and Tanner opened the
window a few inches.

Turning, he looked the room over, because
another thought had occurred to him – perhaps
Chad had not gone out voluntarily. There were still
men on their back trail. Perhaps Charlie Cox hadn't
given it up yet, even Ted Everly, if he had not grown
weary and disgusted with the long trail, could have
found them by now.

'Does that mean anything?' Becky asked as she
stood, unbuttoning the collar button of her flannel
shirt. Tanner looked in the direction of Chad
Garret's rumpled bed where a note lay on the
pillow. Frowning, Tanner walked that way. It could
be anything, an explanation of where Chad had
gone, a ransom demand. He picked up the note
and quickly read the two words scrawled there:

'*Thanks, Partner.*'

Tanner groaned inwardly, then got to his knees to

search under his own bed. There was no sign of the money.

'What's happened?' Becky asked, studying the pained expression on Tanner's face.

'What? I got suckered,' Tanner said, sitting back on his heels. 'I had enough subtle clues; I just didn't want to believe it of Chad.' Stiffly he rose and walked to Becky. He was only a few inches away from her, and her shining blue eyes took him back many years to a point in time when he would have believed her, trusted her about anything.

'What are you going to do?' Becky asked.

'Run the man down,' Tanner said in a low, cold voice. 'I'm sorry, Becky, but you're going to have to stay in this room for a while.'

'I'm tired anyway,' she said, shrugging as if it made no difference to her. Her clear blue eyes which seemed to reflect innocence and deceit depending on Tanner's own mood, shone as she watched him closely.

'I'll be back,' Tanner said. He would have given anything to take her and kiss her, but he would not know who he was kissing – a liar and a thief, or only an image in the moonlight. Tanner grabbed his hat and walked out of the room.

Downstairs in the hotel lobby he leaned against the wall, waiting for his man. It didn't take long.

Across the room he saw a bulky, bearded stranger whose eyes showed he had been drinking, and who wore an expression that said that he had not had enough. Tanner approached him.

'What d'ya want?' the man said in a voice that seemed to rumble from his chest.

'I wanted to offer you a job,' Tanner said to the big stranger. The offer of work obviously didn't appeal to the burly man.

'Stuff that,' he answered.

Tanner fished in his pocket and showed the man a five-dollar gold piece. 'For two minutes work.' The man's dull eyes glittered more brightly than the coin for a minute, then grew wary.

'Who do you want dead?' he asked cautiously.

'It's nothing like that. You don't even have to move from here.' Tanner went on to tell the man what he wanted, and the big man agreed, even smiling toothlessly as Tanner handed over the gold coin.

Upstairs, Tanner returned to the room where Becky sat sagged on Tanner's bed, hands clasped between her knees. She looked up sharply as Tanner entered. Tanner sat beside her for a moment, and told her: 'Becky, I can't let you go with me and I can't leave you alone.'

'You don't trust me?'

'I can't. I trusted Chad Garret, and look where that got me.'

'You're going after this Chad, then?'

'I have to. He's stolen the money I spent many days trying to recover.'

'But you plan to leave me here with Morgan Pride's gold?' Becky asked.

'Why do you ask? Would you try to slip out on me, Becky?'

'Of course not, but what if someone else finds me, finds the gold?'

'I don't think anyone will,' Tanner said seriously as he tried to ignore the sensations that being so near to Becky caused. 'I'm sorry, but you'll have to stay in the room to be safe. The hotel will send up your meals. In the meantime, I've hired a body-guard for you.'

Becky looked doubtfully at him. Tanner continued:

'I don't care what people say about his past, all of those murders – he works for pay – and he is always loyal to the dollar. He won't let anyone get past him and . . . sorry, he won't let you out of your room.'

'But who. . . ?' Becky answered with anxiety showing in her eyes.

'Come with me,' John Tanner said, and he took

her hand to help her to her feet.

Outside, standing in the center of the hotel lobby, a man stood waiting for Tanner to appear on the gallery. When he did, towing a slightly reluctant-looking little blonde with him, the big bearded man did what he had been instructed to do.

Tanner pointed at Becky's head. In response, the bearded stranger pointed back at her and nodded. Then he turned and walked out of the hotel. Five dollars for that kind of work was gravy. And the money was enough for three fresh quarts of whiskey over at the Porcupine.

Tanner thought that the charade had properly impressed Becky. She now seemed willing, even eager, to stay in the room, door locked behind her. For Tanner it was only the beginning of a long tortuous day.

Entering the stable, Tanner still harbored faint hopes that he had been mistaken, but Chad Garret's pinto pony was missing from its stall. The stable man ambled forward to meet Tanner. John asked: 'Have you got a fast animal? I need one.'

'Fast?' the stablehand nodded thoughtfully. 'I've one that was bred as a race horse, but you wouldn't want to know how much it would cost you.'

'I don't want to buy it, just use it for a day or two. Look, these two,' he said indicating his gray and the dun horse Becky had been riding, 'are security for a rental.'

'Both of 'em look pretty beat up,' the man said as he appraised the horses.

'They are – which is why I need to borrow a horse. If I misuse this horse of yours, I'll let you keep these two.'

'Plus fifty dollars.'

'All right,' Tanner said, knowing he was getting taken for a ride. 'Plus fifty dollars.'

The stable man led Tanner to the corral in back of the stable where a big red roan, its coat shining like burnished copper stood watching their approach. 'There he is,' the man said.

'Hell of a good-looking pony,' Tanner said, meaning it.

'It is. I got him from a gambler that got himself trimmed and needed a fresh stake. I figure he bought the horse when he was on a roll.'

'Or won it from someone else.'

'Could be. Anyway, friend, take the roan. You're welcome to it, but if you bring it back foundering it will cost you a lot more than fifty dollars.'

'I just need a fresh horse, something with some speed under me.'

'Hunting someone?'

'Let's just say that a friend of mine left without a

proper goodbye.'

'The gent who was riding that pinto pony?'

'That's the one.'

'I seen you two together; that's why I figured that. He came by an hour or so ago and left like he was in a hurry.'

'Did you see which way he went?' Tanner asked after the stablehand had caught up the roan and begun saddling it.

'I watched him go out. He turned right on Main Street and left town.'

'To the east, you mean?' Tanner asked.

'To the east. Though I don't know why any man would ride out on to that desert unless he had an urgent reason.'

Tanner thought he did: Chad Garret was a desert rat, used to the country, knowing where to find water, how to live off the land. It would be difficult to find Chad in the desert wilderness. Tanner accepted the reins to the tall red roan, swung aboard and started out of town himself, feeling dismal mentally, but he had noticed as he had mounted, remarkably pain-free physically. Damn Chad! Didn't he realize that Tanner would have rewarded him lavishly for the help he had given John? He had even considered taking Chad along with him back to the C-bar-C where Chad could find honest work and a decent home. And he could have used Chad's capable help on the trail. Apparently the thought of the stolen gold just across the room was too much for Chad to resist.

Tanner understood the impulse, but Chad Garret was not going to keep the loot. John had worked too hard, ridden too far to give Ben Canasta's hard-earned money away now.

He rode the wide desert once again, feeling the fine-lined, sleek pony he was riding moving smoothly beneath him. About a mile out of town he decided to test the horse and heeled it to a full gallop. It was like riding a lightning bolt once the roan reached full stride, and John slowed the horse again. It might have to be ridden far. There was no telling. The sun was still high, white in the crystal-blue sky. He remembered Chad Garret's own rule about riding through the heat of the day, and wondered if that rule applied when you were riding with your saddle-bags filled with another man's money.

John Tanner was already perspiring heavily after an hour in the kiln of the desert. The red roan had slowed noticeably, its eagerness fading. John rode on, taking the miles carefully – half of each mile at a walk, the other half at a canter. When he slowed the roan to a walk, his face was surrounded by blow-flies: a sign that there was something recently dead in the vicinity, for the nasty things lay their eggs in dead flesh or in the wounds of living creatures.

How far was he from the wash where he and Chad had once rested? There was no telling; he only knew that men, like all other animals, are creatures of habit, returning to places they have once had safety and comfort.

The one sure thing was that Chad would have to rest sometime; his pinto could not be in that good a shape, even with the brief rest it had had in Ruidoso. There John definitely had the advantage. The roan had not been ridden for a long while, and it was fresh and perky. Where Chad had the large advantage was in his knowledge of the country. John was lost, he realized. He had had enough sense to fill a burlap waterbag and he would not go dry for sometime. The horse was a different matter.

The sun lowered itself slowly toward the far, chocolate-colored mountains, but it had grown no cooler. The white sand was stained pink by the setting sun, but there was no shade to be found, not a breath of air stirred.

Abruptly John saw, thought he saw, a dust cloud on the distant horizon. With no wind blowing, he concluded that it had to be a horse kicking up dust in its passing. How many men could there be out here on the open desert riding on this day? Damned few, and he lifted the red roan into a canter again.

He had caught up with his man.

Now the sky began to darken noticeably as the sun began to hide its face behind the hills. There was a coolness across the land as the day sank into shadow. Welcome as it was, the coolness was a harbinger of the settling darkness. Tanner hurried on. What chance would he have of finding Chad Garret in the desert night?

The roan mis-stepped and stumbled and Tanner cursed. He could not lose the horse to a broken leg. A man out here without a horse was as condemned to death as a prisoner waiting on the scaffold for his executioner. He slowed the animal again to a walk, letting it pick its own way across the ground which had now begun to be broken, red sand desert.

He cursed Chad Garret three or four times, but it did nothing to help him gain ground, did nothing to alleviate his fury. The moon was already rising in the east; the orb resembled a gaunt ghostly face. Hadn't he seen such a moon before?

The land began to lift and roll now, and the figure he thought he had seen disappeared behind a sandy knoll, but as Tanner crested a rise, he could see the man on horseback, much nearer now, the crazy moon silhouetting him. Tanner dipped into a small valley and scaled another knoll. The man ahead of him was still nearer now, his horse seemed to be faltering, and Tanner decided to test the roan's speed. He heeled it into startled motion, and its muscles uncoiled like taut springs. If that was Chad Garret ahead, and it had to be, he could not give the desert rat time to find one of his hideouts.

The roan continued to run swiftly, with apparent ease as Tanner raced toward the moon and his mounted prey. The night was cool, the roan's hoofs sent up sprays of sand as it charged up yet another knoll and dipped down again. Now the man ahead of Tanner did see him coming. He sat his horse – it was a pinto – for a moment, just staring in disbelief, and then slapped spurs to the spotted pony. Tanner recognized the man's hat, the red shirt he had been wearing, and he rode on wildly. The pinto had little left to give after the long trail it had run, and it slowed despite its owner's urging, finally coming to a dead stop. Exhausted, quivering, the pinto could run no farther. Tanner's fresh red roan drove on. John watched as Chad Garret leaped from the saddle, hurriedly untied the saddle-bags from his horse's back and raced off madly.

Where Chad thought he was going, there was no telling. But he was not going to outrace a running horse on this open land. Chad slowed and turned, firing across his shoulder at the charging Tanner.

He must have known who it was, who it had to be, still John felt a pang of sorrow that his new friend would actually shoot at him. Tanner had a rifle in his scabbard and thought he could probably pull up the roan and shoot Chad down.

The thing was, he could not. Chad had pulled his irons out of the fire on more than one occasion. He decided to try it another way.

'Chad?' he called out. 'Just give me the money back – that's all I want. Drop your saddle-bags and I'll let you walk away from this.'

Chad was on one knee, his face bone-white in the light of the moon, his pistol aimed and steady. He shouted out a muffled curse and pulled the trigger on his pistol. Tanner ducked reflexively as the shot was fired, although by the time he heard the report of the gun, the bullet, of course, had already flown past. His horse was rearing up and shaking its head angrily. Chad's bullet had gone through the roan's left ear.

That was too close to allow for further consideration. Chad was trying for a killing shot, and Tanner reached for his rifle as he tried to settle the angry, nervous roan. By the time he unsheathed the Winchester, Chad had risen to his feet again, and he now held his Colt with both hands. He meant to kill Tanner; there was no doubt about that now.

'Chad?' Tanner yelled again, shouldering his rifle at the same time. He saw the flame explode from the barrel of the Colt, saw Chad's face illuminated brightly as the shot rang out. Then Tanner sent a spinning .44-40 bullet into Chad's chest, saw the man flop back against the sand and lie unmoving in the silver-gray moonlight.

There was no room left in Tanner's heart for regret. He had killed the man only because it had been necessary for his own survival. Swinging down from his saddle he walked slowly toward the still figure of Chad Garret. Garret was definitely dead. His saddle-bags lay inches away from his nerveless hand. His eyes were still open, staring skyward. Tanner was not sorry that Chad was dead, only that a thing so small as the twitching of a finger could end a life like that; in one brief second erase the friendship they had shared on the long trail.

John took no more time to speculate on the workings of his own mind, his burdened soul. He unsaddled the pinto, slipped its bit and tossed the reins aside, then he clambered aboard the roan and started back toward Ruidoso, hoping that Becky Canasta had been effectively managed and that she had not somehow broken free to cause more trouble.

SEVEN

It remained cold; the star-bright sky was still and haunting as John Tanner retraced his steps and halted the roan in front of the stable in Ruidoso. He called out twice, three times then waited patiently. The stable hand would have undoubtedly been asleep at this hour; although his duties required him to respond at any hour to any traveler needing assistance, he would not be happy to be dragged from his bed.

After much grumbling, the man appeared, his thumb hooked under one red suspender, adjusting it over his shoulder.

'Oh, it's you,' he said by way of greeting.

'Afraid so. Hated to wake you up, but we have some business.'

'Hey,' the stableman said, suddenly becoming

alert as he reached up to stroke the roan's neck. 'What's this – he's been shot in the ear.'

'Yes, he has,' Tanner said wearily. 'You'd better tend to it.'

'I will, by God! Then I'll tend to you. Brother, you will pay for this.'

'What's the going price on a horse's ear?' Tanner asked.

'Well, I don't know,' the man sputtered. 'But you'll pay.'

'I will pay,' Tanner promised.

'Beautiful animal like that,' the man griped, his voice falling to a low muttering as he unsaddled the roan and put it up. Tanner took a few minutes to look at his gray horse which eyed him uneasily as if suspecting that his human meant to take him out to get his ear shot now. Tanner patted the gray and then walked back to the front of the stable where by lantern-light he completed his deal with the stable hand, apparently to the man's satisfaction.

It was just past midnight when Tanner, bone-weary and unhappy walked toward the hotel, saddle-bag over his shoulder. He supposed he should take another room now, but first he meant to check on Becky. She might have decided the false bodyguard had been just that, simply packed her bags and walked out of the room. But she had been obviously frightened and weary, so Tanner did not really think she would have attempted anything on that night. But he was determined to take nothing for granted from then on.

With a tap, Tanner proceeded into the hotel room, relieved to find Becky where he had left her. The phantom bodyguard had done his job, it seemed. Tanner slid his saddle-bags under his bed and sat down, looking at Becky's pale, wary face. Nothing could be read from her expression.

'What are you doing?' she asked as Tanner tugged his boots off.

'I am going to sleep,' he replied.

'In here – with me?'

'Yes.' Tanner stretched out on the bed, still dressed. He couldn't remember a comfort greater than that of having a mattress to stretch out on. His body felt shaken, battered and trail-weary. He was lucky – by then he could have felt quite dead.

'I don't like you sleeping here,' Becky protested. 'Besides, I've been cooped up in here for a long time. I could use some fresh air.'

'Open the window.'

Tanner curled up. He was bone-tired and knew he would sleep deeply, but not so deeply that Becky could slip past him – if she had such an idea in mind. Besides, she did not know if the ugly bearded man was still out there, watching. After half an hour or so, Tanner heard Becky shift on her bed, and he forced himself to stay awake until the movement on her bed stopped and he heard her soft steady breathing. Then he allowed himself four hours of heavy, dreamless sleep.

The first golden glint of sunrise struck the hotel window and brought Tanner instantly awake. He felt refreshed but his thoughts were a muddle as he sat on the side of his bed, hands clenched. Becky Canasta was there, still asleep, and the money – almost all of it – was there as well. He stamped into his boots, making no effort to be quiet, then walked to the basin on the bureau, splashed in some water from the ewer and rinsed off as well as he could, avoiding his image in the stained mirror.

'It's so early,' Becky said as she sat up.

'And it will be hot before long. Get your riding clothes on, Becky; we're heading home to the C-bar-C.'

'Why are you in such a rush!' she complained behind a yawn.

'Because this is as close as I've been,' he explained. 'Every time I think I've taken a step forward, I find that I've been pushed two steps back. Aren't you eager to get home? To see your father?'

'Of course,' she said a little snippily, 'but I can't

see that a few hours, a day matters much.'

'Your father may only have a few days, a few hours,' Tanner told her. She nodded thoughtfully, and he said, 'I'm going down to the restaurant to get some coffee for us. I'll only be gone a few minutes, but that should give you time to dress.' At the doorway, he paused and said: 'I can see the room from the restaurant.'

Becky's expression hardened. 'I suppose that means you don't trust me, not at all. I don't see why not.'

'When we have a lot of time, I'll tell you,' he answered before going out the door and down the stairs to the restaurant.

The man at the stable was a different one – perhaps the owner. Tanner told him what they had come for and he checked his ledger and took another few dollars from Tanner. Thinking how much he had spent at these places, Tanner thought that it might be a good business to be in. After all, anyone riding the desert eventually needed feed and water for his mount.

Tanner managed to saddle his own gray with little difficulty. Then he helped Becky with her dun, tying her travelling bag to the saddle pommel. On this morning she was oddly cheerful. Perhaps she had managed to sleep away her thoughts of the kidnapping, whatever terror Morgan Pride might have put in her heart.

The gray was heavily burdened with the weight of the three saddle-bags, but he was still reluctant to use Becky's dun for carrying a portion of the stolen money. Perhaps his suspicions were unfounded, after all this was Becky Canasta! Still he gave her only the water bag to carry, tied to the opposite side of the saddlehorn to balance the weight of the traveling bag.

The sun was low, raking their eyes as they rode out of Ruidoso, once again to attempt the long desert. John Tanner thought that he should feel uplifted, with his task nearly completed, but he did not. A vague uneasiness, an even vaguer longing settled over him as he walked the gray across the red desert, the sun rising with incredible slowness. The horses seemed to move through wet cement, the hours felt like weeks, months, years as they passed in painful progression And course it grew hotter, still hotter. Tanner envied Ben Canasta his ranch in the pine forest; the old man had chosen wisely when he settled there. Perhaps, Tanner thought, he could find a place like that for himself and. . . .

He reined in his fantastic thoughts. He had only known Candice Grant for a few days, those spent as if she were nursing an injured animal. He knew little about the young lady who owned the hat shop, nothing of what she intended to do, wished for, hoped to have one day. It likely didn't involve a rambling man who owned nothing.

'You couldn't have believed her,' Becky Canasta said out of the dead silence.

'Believe who?' he asked, briefly thinking that Becky had somehow penetrated his daydream.

'Monique, of course,' Becky said rather sharply. 'You can't have believed her when she told you that I voluntarily assisted Morgan Pride in that robbery. My father's money! It would have been mine someday anyway.'

'Some people don't like waiting for that day to come,' Tanner said, squinting at her through the sun rays.

'It was only because Monique wanted Matt Doyle!' an exasperated Becky exclaimed. 'He wanted me, but I did not want him. But Matt kept playing up to me and Monique developed a heated jealousy.'

'I know that,' Tanner said, because that much was true. But there had to be more to it. Not many women would shoot a man just because he was paying her unwanted attention. What was the real reason Becky had shot Matt Doyle? John might

111

never learn that.

He might never learn anything about Becky Canasta at all.

They rode on. Occasionally Tanner looked across his shoulder. Would Charlie Cox and Wes Dalton take up the pursuit again? It seemed not, but there was a lot of money involved. This was their last chance to recover it – out on the open desert with no witnessing eyes for mile after mile. There was no telling, anymore than there was about the intentions of Ted Everly and his crew, sent after Morgan Pride by Monique with instructions to bring Beck Canasta home to the C-bar-C.

Tanner had been riding the trail a long time. Now it seemed that the trails in his mind were just as confused and lost as those he followed. He focused his thoughts again and set his mind on the things he could accomplish and did not need to understand – he would take Ben Canasta's daughter and his money to the old man. After that he would be finished with the C-bar-C and all of its closely-held secrets.

He owed them nothing more – none of them.

By noon the high sky sun had begun to take its toll. Mirages had begun to form wispy threads of substanceless images before Tanner's eyes. He squinted into the sun, trying to clear his warped vision. Glancing at Becky, he could see that she had gotten worn down as well. She slumped in the saddle, leaning over her dun's withers.

They needed anything – a hint of shadow, a flickering tongue of cool breeze to keep them going. There was nothing.

And then there was or so his glare-ravaged eyes suggested. Tanner saw a long line of gray vegetation to his left. It must be, had to be the dry wash where he had first encountered Chad Garret, where they had rested in the heated shade of the willows. He tried to shout out to Becky, but his voice was a strangled croak. Eventually Tanner got her attention and pointed out the long line of dead willow trees. It was not certain if she understood their significance or not, but she followed him across the sand toward the shallow wash. Reaching it, Tanner led the way, his horse sliding down the bluff, going nearly to its haunches.

Again there was no obvious sign of water along the bottom of the coulee, but here and there Tanner noticed that some of the shaggy old trees had bright green young leaves at their extremities. The two of them did not need water just then; they still carried the burlap waterbag they had brought from Ruidoso. They needed first of all shade and a place to rest. Later Tanner would scout around and try to find standing water for the horses.

Across the dry riverbed, Tanner spotted a decent-sized copse. Not much, but it would have to do. He started across the streambed; Becky followed without a signal passing between them.

'Thank God,' she gasped as she swung down from her dun horse's back. 'I don't think I could have ridden on for another hour.'

They spread their saddle blankets on the sand beneath the willows leaving their disappointed horses to search out whatever poor foliage they could discover. The shade was thin, the air still and hot, but it was some respite from the stunning heat of the desert day. Sagging, Tanner sat on his blanket as gnats and deer flies swarmed around them. A stream of red ants made its way across the white sand of the river bottom, going somewhere known only to them. Otherwise the earth was silent and still.

Tanner glanced at Becky and saw that she had already stretched out, arm thrown over her eyes, trying to sleep. Tanner leaned back himself, knowing that there was nothing useful to be done just then, and that he had to take this opportunity to rest while he could. They still had a long ride to Split Rock and from there back to the C-bar-C. He could will himself to hurry on, to get back to the home ranch, but he knew he did not have the physical resources just then, and so he let his eyelids close, and slept if uncomfortably, restoringly.

When Tanner next awoke it was with a start, with a sense of disorientation. He sat up, taking long minutes to clear his mind, to remember where he was. Becky still lay sprawled nearby. Perspiration glistened on her forehead and upper lip. Tanner was aware now of a stirring breeze in the willows, and glancing to the west he could see that the sun was dropping toward the far horizon. How long had he slept? It did not matter – he had needed the sleep. They were no longer in a race no matter how eager each might have been to get back to the C-bar-C. Where. . . .

Where what? Where anything might have happened in their absence. Ben Canasta might have passed away. Monique might be in charge of things. Ted Everly might have made his way back to the ranch.

It was too much to think about. Tanner rose heavily, unkinking his back. Looking again at Becky, he decided to spend some time searching the river bottom for a pool of standing water where the horses could drink. Plugging his hat on, he walked northward, leading his gray. The dun decided to stand where it was. At least the horse would be some reassurance for Becky should she wake up confused and feeling deserted.

Tanner did find water – in a blundering way. Walking through the willow brush, his forearm held up to fend off the dry twigs, he stepped right into a shallow pond. Muttering a small curse he stepped quickly aside and led the horse forward. The gray dipped its muzzle into the pond, found the water palatable and proceeded to drink its fill while Tanner watched, seated in the shade.

Deciding that he had better see that Becky's dun was watered if they were to travel on that evening, he started to rise to return to the camp. Just as he was getting to his feet, a pistol fired near at hand. Tanner hit the ground, seeing no one nearby. The bullet must have been slightly deflected by a twig on a low-growing willow, for it only stung his cheek and sang off into the brush. Either that or the gunman had been a poor shot.

Crouched defensively, Colt in his hand, Tanner saw a shadowy figure darting away from the pond. Apparently the man had no stomach for a face to face fight. It was chancy, but Tanner took aim at the fleeing man, led him slightly and fired his .44. There was a small grunt and then a crash of brush as Tanner's bullet tagged home. Carefully Tanner crept through the tangle of dust-covered willow brush, his eyes alert to any movement, any small sound. Blood trickled down from his cheek which had now begun to burn savagely.

Tanner moved on, one step at a time, wiping the perspiration from his eyes. No breeze stirred in the close confines of the canyon.

He found the man curled up and unmoving a few dozen yards on. He rolled the gunman over with his toe and crouched down beside him. The dead man was narrowly-built and wore a drooping black mustache. Tanner didn't know his name, but he had been one of the men who had sided with Ted Everly back at the C-bar-C.

That could only mean that Everly was nearby. Tanner sighed. He should have taken more pains to leave no clear tracks on the desert. He had thought that he had enough lead that it was not necessary. He figured that the end of the trail was near enough that it made no difference. He should have already learned that there was no end to this trail.

Rising, he started back the way he had come, gun in his hand. He passed the gray horse without collecting its reins. He did not need the big oaf crashing through the brush behind him. Tanner approached the camp silently, his eyes alert to every shadow.

The dun horse was not where he had left it.

Becky Canasta was gone.

Perhaps, he thought, she had heard the shot, panicked when she did not see Tanner around and ridden out on to the desert on her own. That was the best alternative, but it was not what had happened. In the soft sand it was easy enough to see the tracks of two other horses in the camp. Ted Everly – it had to be. Tanner looked around just long enough to discover the earthen ramp formed where a section of bluff had collapsed and formed a path leading up out of the dry wash. There three sets of horse tracks followed one another up to the desert, heading east toward Split Rock.

At least they were headed in the direction Tanner wanted to go. There were deeper shadows beneath the willows now, and he glanced westward toward the descending sun, calculating how much daylight remained. Then he collected the reins to his patient gray horse and began to follow the party of riders ahead of him.

EIGHT

The night was still young, but the temperature had dropped precipitously. The gray horse slogged on at an even pace. Here is where Tanner had the advantage, or so he believed. The gray had been used sparingly over the past few days, and now it had been watered well. Becky's little dun must be worn down, and so probably were those of Ted Everly and the other man riding with him – whoever he was. Tanner felt sure that he was gaining ground on them. Split Rock was not that far off now.

The silver moon hung low on the horizon like an observing eye as he continued to move eastward. Now and then Tanner glanced behind him, because you never knew. The man he had shot in the gully would not be following, nor did he think Charlie Cox or Wes Dalton would be. The two were both strangers in a strange town, and Tanner could not see them raising a gang without money to pay them. Neither seemed up to it. That just left the two men riding ahead of him, returning Becky Canasta to the C-bar-C. For whom? Certainly Ben Canasta could not have sent them. That meant that it was Monique who had wanted Becky brought back – and Tanner himself. For what purpose? Monique hated both of them, blamed them for Matt Doyle's death on that summer night. Could she have held that grudge for so long?

Certainly.

Ahead now Tanner could see the monolith which was Split Rock jutting into the starry sky. Further along he began to smell pine scent, and straining his eyes he could make out a ridge which had separated itself from the mountains, like an island on the desert where pine trees grew cutting serrated silhouettes against the moonlit sky. Closer and closer – it was hard to believe he had finally made it back this close to the C-bar-C. In fact he could just tag along and let Becky be returned to the ranch, but would Ben Canasta even be aware of Becky's return if Ted Everly delivered Becky to Monique. The dark eyed woman was mad with vengeance – that much she had made clear to Tanner. No, Tanner had to recapture the girl before they reached the ranch.

He lifted the gray's pace a little, scanning the wide land as he approached the stone monument.

He saw no firelight, saw no standing horses, but perhaps they were on the eastern side of the huge rock. He slowed the gray again. He was positive that the travelers would pause before the last leg of the trip. Simply because he knew the condition their horses must be in. The dun, in particular, had already been ridden nearly into the ground.

He moved along the moon-shadowed trail past stands of mesquite and nopal cactus, leaving it to the gray to find the way as he slicked his rifle from its scabbard, listening to and watching the night.

Tanner decided to circle the bulk of Split Rock from the north, his left. It was the way less used. Stillness blanketed the night as he walked the gray carefully around the towering rock. And then he heard it – a horse nickered somewhere not far ahead of him, around the shoulder of the land-form. Grinning, his mouth tight, teeth clenched, Tanner continued on. He could feel the warmth of the day accumulated by the huge rock.

John Tanner heard a voice – or believed he did – and then inching ahead, saw the vague golden light of a dying fire. He rounded the shoulder of the towering rock and a rifle cracked, breaking the stillness of the night. John's horse drew up, staggered and then rolled. Tanner had barely enough time to kick free of the stirrups, losing his rifle as he leaped from the saddle. Then he scrambled rapidly away from the horse whose thrashing hoofs struck out wildly as it flailed through its reflexive death run.

The night returned to silence. Tanner lay next to the base of Split Rock, trying to still his breathing. Even the pulse of his blood sounded loud in his ears. He had not been as silent or as clever as he had thought. He had lost his hat; his hair hung in his eyes. He had lost his Winchester; his Colt was clenched tightly in his perspiring hand. He could hear cautious boot steps whispering across the sand, approaching cautiously.

One man or two? He thought only one. He rolled on to his belly, braced himself on his elbows and cocked his revolver. His eyes picked out one low star and he kept his eyes focused on it. It shone silver-bright and then blinked off as a figure pass in front of it and Tanner fired three shots in a row, the smoke curling past his head, stinging his eyes and nostrils. There was a grunt and a thud and the star beamed on again.

Whoever the man had been, he would not be rising again, Tanner knew. There was no point in remaining where he was, and so he began crawling forward, the rough ground tearing at his elbows and knees. He heard a muted, urgent whispering and then the sounds of creaking saddle leather, and incautiously John got to his feet and rushed around the shoulder of the rock. By the light of the small, dying campfire, he saw a man swinging his leg up and over a black horse's back. From the corner of his eye he saw Becky, sitting on her dun horse, looking weary and defeated, but he forced himself to concentrate on the man riding the black.

'Everly!' he yelled, and Ted Everly tried to do too many things at once.

Instead of just lining his horse out of there, which is what he should have done, Everly tried to control his horse, turn in the saddle, draw his gun and find a target for his pistol sights. By the time he finally located Tanner's shadow pressed against the rock, it was already too late for Ted Everly. The two men's shots were only a split second apart, but Tanner had been braced and ready while Everly had been trying to control his horse and fire across his shoulder. Everly's bullet rang off the face of the rock and spattered Tanner with red dust before ricocheting away into the vastness of the desert.

Tanner's bullet struck home.

The black horse reared up as Tanner's bullet knocked Everly from the saddle. Then it circled warily, confused by the commotion. Tanner approached Ted Everly's still form, but he didn't need to take much of a look – Everly was dead.

Rising, Tanner took the black horse's reins in his hand and stroked the horse's neck, trying to soothe it.

Becky Canasta stood silhouetted by the golden glow of the dying campfire. Her hands were clasped, her head slightly lowered. She looked smaller somehow, pitiable. Her eyes, when she lifted them to John's, were damp. He could not differentiate which expressions of hers were sincere, which simply dressing. He vowed that he would no longer try, that he no longer cared, although he was not quite being honest with himself. A little more gruffly than was necessary, he told her:

'Get your horse ready. We're riding home.'

'Tonight?' she asked in a weary voice.

'Tonight. I'm taking you back where you belong.'

They rode on then into the face of the coming moon. Becky's little dun moved on steadily, almost eagerly despite its recent trials. Ted Everly's tall black horse had an uncertain gait. Tanner thought he knew why that was. The long-legged animal was probably used to a high-stepping pace, but now, out of weariness, it didn't seem to have the vigor required for that sort of traveling.

Now the ridge to John's left stood out starkly

against the night sky, a row of pines along its crest. They were close to the C-bar-C, very close. He glanced at Becky, but her face was expressionless. He wondered what thoughts were in her mind, but was glad that he did not know. Silently they made their way toward Ben Canasta's ranch house. John wondered if the old man were still alive, or if all of this had been for nothing.

Tanner smelled smoke before he saw it rising in a nearly straight line from the main house. Both of the horses pricked up their ears and tried to hasten their pace. Home: they could smell it, hear their horse-friends, scent water and hay. They slowed the eager horses and rode directly toward the front of the house. They walked the horses through the huge oaks in the yard. There were no sounds near the house, nor from the bunkhouse.

When the figure appeared suddenly in front of them, the black halted sharply without Tanner's command.

'It's about time you got back here!' the shadowed figure yelled. 'I thought you'd run off to Mexico.'

Now peering through the shadows, Tanner made her out – Monique. She had recognized Becky's pale hair, the dun she rode, and likewise recognized Ted Everly's tall black horse. But with Tanner's face shadowed by the brim of his hat, she had not recognized him, and naturally enough, took Tanner for Ted Everly.

'Have you got a gun, Monique?' Tanner asked.

'Of course not. What do I need a . . . who are you!'

'Tanner. Why don't you let us pass? I mean to see Ben Canasta.'

'It's late,' Monique said, nervousness causing her voice to grow taut, raising it a pitch.

'I know it is,' Tanner said. 'But I've been riding long and hard with only one goal in mind – to return to Ben what's his. We're passing now – I hope I don't hear you calling out for anyone's help.'

'What would be the point?' Monique said in a softer, defeated voice. She turned and started back toward the house, her skirts dusting the ground.

Ben Canasta was awake, but barely as Tanner knocked on the door to his bedroom and found the man, propped up on pillows, staring into the conscience of the night. His watery eyes flickered toward Tanner, startled.

'John! What's happened? Did you. . . .'

Then Becky emerged from the shadows of the hallway, walked past Tanner and went to her father's bedside to kneel, her head resting on his chest as he stroked her tangled pale hair. Tanner retreated to the hallway and seated himself on a bench of dark wood inlaid with ceramics. He kept the saddle-bags between his boots.

A half an hour or less elapsed before Becky emerged from the old man's bedroom, her eyes seeming triumphant.

'He wants to see you now,' Becky said, and there seemed to be a hint of warning in her words. Tanner shrugged the impression off; probably he was imagining it. He had done nothing but imagine things about Becky Canasta since he had met her.

Shouldering the three saddle-bags he tramped into Ben Canasta's bedroom. The old man still sat, propped up on his pillows. His watery eyes watched Tanner's movements gravely. John found himself wondering what Becky had told her father. He supposed it didn't matter anymore, none of it. He dropped the saddle-bags on the floor beside a red-plush upholstered chair and sat on it, tilting his hat back curiously.

'Is that all of it, John?' Ben asked as if it made no difference to him.

'Except for what they spent and what I needed to travel on. I really never had a reason to count it.'

'That's fine,' Ben said, letting his eyes close. 'And you brought my Becky back to me. I owe you more than you will ever know, John.'

'You're welcome to my time, Ben. I'm only happy

that it's all over with.'

'I hope it is,' Ben Canasta said in a low voice. 'If only . . . my daughters could get along, I could die in peace.'

Daughters?

John gave voice to his question. 'Ben, do you mean that Becky and. . . .'

'Yes, Becky and Monique are sisters. Half-sisters, really. I have been twice married.'

That made the antagonism between the two somewhat clearer. Ben went on as if talking while he was half-asleep. Perhaps his thoughts were bogged down in the swamps of his past. 'They never got along, you know. Monique always figured that I favored Becky – I don't know! Maybe I did. If so, I should have never let it show.'

'Matt Doyle,' Tanner suggested.

'Yes,' Ben sighed, opening his eyes again. 'They both wanted him. Maybe he wanted both of them. Monique thought that her sister had set her eyes on her man, the one thing she possessed that Becky couldn't have. Something like that. I don't understand women, and they never confided in me. After you shot Matt Doyle, Monique went a little over the edge. I'm ashamed to say that I didn't see it. Not that I could have done much about it.'

'I'm afraid,' he said with a deep sigh, 'that

Monique set out to avenge herself on Becky by having her kidnapped by that loathsome Morgan Pride, rewarding him with the money from my safe.'

Tanner nodded. Although what Ben was saying made sense in a logical way, still it didn't seem to ring true to Tanner who at the same time had to admit that he didn't know Becky that well, Monique not at all. He rose from the chair.

'Where should I put the money for tonight?' John asked. Ben Canasta looked indifferent.

'Kick it under my bed, John. I'll put it in the safe in the morning.'

'That's not very secure,' Tanner pointed out.

'What is?' Ben Canasta asked wearily. 'Don't you see, John, it just doesn't matter anymore.'

'All right,' John Tanner agreed. He managed a joke which caused the old man's lips to twitch with slight amusement. 'But if it comes up missing again – don't call me.'

'Get yourself something to eat, John. Then find yourself a bed in the bunkhouse.'

'I'm much more weary than hungry, sir,' Tanner said, 'and if you don't mind, I'll just find myself a place in the barn to sleep.'

'You still think you have enemies here?' Ben asked.

'Let's just say that I don't intend to find out.'

Ben Canasta didn't answer; he was already asleep. Tanner went out, closing the door softly behind him. He saw no one else awake in the house or out in the yard. He gathered up the reins to the black horse and to Becky's little dun and led them toward the barn through the silky shadows the moon cast beneath the oak trees.

It was a labor of the mind rather than of the body to see that the horses were taken care of before he crawled up the wooden ladder to the hayloft where he pulled together a pile of hay which he half-tumbled on to to take his long-awaited rest.

The morning sun was a brilliant array of shafting sun rays in the old barn. There were a few men Tanner didn't know stamping around below, preparing their horses for their day's work, grumbling in the usual manner of men roused at an early hour to face grueling tasks. Tanner sat still, letting his head clear as the cowhands muttered and cursed, saddled their ponies and went out to encounter the new day.

When they were gone, John started down the ladder, hunger gnawing at his stomach. Carefully, almost secretively, he made his way across the yard and then to the back of the house where he knew the kitchen door to be. There would be no hands inside – they were all fed in the bunkhouse – and so he went in, hearing the door creak on its brass hinges, and seated himself at the table, holding his head in his hands. Despite all the battering his body had taken over the last few days he did not feel bruised and sore, only tired, incredibly so. What was that called? The French he knew, had a word for it, but before he could find it, the inner door opened and, carrying a tray of dishes, Monique entered the kitchen.

' 'Morning,' Tanner mumbled, getting no response from the dark eyed woman, but only a side-long disparaging glance.

John watched as Monique, in a black dress and white apron, slid the dirty breakfast dishes from the tray into the steel sink. She leaned against the sink, hands braced there and stared out the small window over it as if she were waiting for someone, something. But there would never again be something, someone to wait for.

'Any chance of getting a cup of coffee?' John asked, feeling as if he were intruding on her kitchen, her thoughts, her life.

'Sure,' Monique said more lightly than the expression in her eyes reflected. 'Wait and I'll fry up some ham and eggs for you too. After all – I've been thinking about it, John you were only a dupe, like the rest of us.'

Tanner's gunbelt was cutting at his waist. It seemed that he had been wearing it forever, and it was hardly considered proper wear at a breakfast table. He rose, unbuckled the weight of the Colt and hung it on one of a row of pegs on the wall behind him. Monique brought him coffee in a blue ceramic cup and walked away. John watched the steam from the coffee curlicue up into the cool morning air of the kitchen.

'What sort of dupe?' he asked. He found himself still wanting to know, needing to separate fact from fiction. He had been told so many stories from different perspectives that he remained as confused as ever when he tried sorting things out.

'Look.' Monique said as she began scrubbing the dishes in the sink with a brass brush. 'For starters, I know that you did not kill Matt Doyle. It was Becky, wasn't it? Never mind – I already know the answer. What kind of dupe would allow himself to be sent to prison for something he did not do? And, Tanner, you didn't know then that they might not hang you for it! For what – a glimpse of a petticoat?' She smiled faintly. 'Yes, that is what I would call a dupe.'

'So you decided to take your revenge on Becky?' Tanner asked. 'Staging the robbery, having her captured and brought back here so that you could . . .

what did you have planned for her, Monique?'

'You still can't see everything like it was, can you? I rob my own father? Do you think. . . ?'

It was at that moment that the kitchen door swung open and Becky Canasta swept into the room.

NINE

The two women glared at one another. There was no sound in the room, but it seemed as if two hissing cats were stalking each other as each woman took a cautious step forward. The hatred was palpable.

'Father would like another cup of coffee,' Becky said finally, holding out a mug toward her half-sister. Monique's voice was even colder than Becky's had been.

'Pour it yourself. You do know how to do a simple job like that, don't you? Or do you save your cunning for things like cracking safes?'

'Now you're accusing me of that, too!' Becky yelled. 'I know that you took it and had me kidnapped so that I couldn't tell Father.'

'You know it, do you! You little liar!' Monique

answered. Neither of them had so much as glanced at Tanner, but he had the feeling that they were playing out the scene for his benefit. 'You paid Morgan Pride to abduct me.'

'You wanted to ride off with him,' Monique countered.

'Oh, yes! Was he supposed to return and give you half of the stolen money, Monique? I think so. And then when he didn't you sent Ted Everly after him, didn't you?'

'You're a liar, and you always will be a liar!' Monique shouted. 'You always had everything while I became a scullery maid.' Her eyes turned briefly down. 'Once I had a chance. . . .'

'With Matt Doyle,' Becky shot back with scornful harshness. 'He was only using you – for what I can only guess. He loved me, you ugly little fool!'

That was enough for Monique. She grabbed the long, well-honed knife she had been using to slice the ham and lunged toward Becky Canasta. Tanner rolled out of his chair to get out of the way. As he did he saw Becky go to the gunbelt he had left hanging on the wall, and before he could rise, he heard the report of the .44, its violent roar terrific in the close room. Smoke layered the kitchen ceiling. Becky dropped the pistol and stood shuddering, hands to her face. Monique lay on her back against the floor, one leg bent under her, a look of surprise on her face, pale with death.

Tanner leveraged himself to his feet and walked toward Becky.

'She came at me with the knife! You saw it, John. You did see it all, didn't you?'

Her eyes were pleading as she gripped his arms. When she looked past Tanner to study her dead sister's body, Tanner saw nothing in her teary eyes. Tears could be produced, but not the empty, somehow gloating expression in those blue eyes. The door behind them burst open and Ben Canasta in a red dressing gown appeared, his gaze going from Becky to Tanner, to Monique.

'My God!' the old man said, his legs trembling. Tanner righted the chair on the floor and helped Canasta to sit. 'John, did you. . . ?'

'I did it!' Becky said, There seemed to be a hint of pride in her voice, but the tears continued to flow, and she went to sit on her father's lap, throwing her arms around his neck. 'She came at me with a carving knife. Isn't that so, John!'

'It's so,' Tanner had to admit.

'But why. . . ?' Ben Canasta asked feebly. It was too much for him to take in. Probably he would spend the rest of his life wondering.

Tanner stooped and picked up his Colt. As he

reached to remove his holster and belt from the peg, three C-bar-C men, summoned by the shot, burst into the kitchen. They started for Tanner, but Ben Canasta kept them back.

'It's not what it seems, boys.'

That didn't satisfy the cowhands, Tanner knew as he studied their expressions, their angry eyes. They knew Tanner only as a killer, an outsider. Nevertheless for the moment, they backed out of the kitchen.

Becky sat on her father's lap still, clinging to his neck as her meaningless tears ran down her cheeks. Tanner strapped on his gun and retrieved his hat.

'I'll be on my way, Ben, unless you need me to. . . .' He looked to where Monique lay.

'No I don't need you for that,' Ben said wearily. 'But, John, why go? The men around here now don't know you. They've just heard all of the rumors. Once they get to know you . . . you could have a good home on the ranch, John, a comfortable life.'

Becky lifted her head just long enough to look at John Tanner and he decided – he could never be comfortable on the C-bar-C or around Becky Canasta. He had already cared for her two years too long.

'I thank you, Ben, but I can't,' he said. 'If you

would let me have a horse. . . .'

'Any mount you see with the C-bar-C brand is yours,' Ben said, his voice still shaky. 'John . . . for everything you tried to do, I thank you.'

It seemed that there should be much more to say, but nothing occurred to Tanner just then. He took one last look at the pathetic tableaux and then went out, closing the door, leaving the memory of it behind.

Exiting the house into bright sunlight he saw the two surly-looking cowhands standing on the far end of the porch. John was in no mood for trouble. He had had enough; he only wanted to get clear of the C-bar-C and out on to the clean, open desert. He walked directly toward them heading for the barn.

'Out of my ways, boys, or there won't be enough men left to bury the survivors.'

It was still cool inside the barn at this time of the morning. Tanner took his time looking over the horses there, finally choosing a thick-muscled stubby buckskin horse with a white star on its muzzle and an ornery glint in its eye. He had learned enough to know that he did not want a long-legged, high-stepping animal to cross the desert on.

He took Ted Everly's saddle, knowing that the

man had no further use for it, and had just finished tightening the cinches when a young Mexican boy, no more than nine or ten years old, came in with a pair of saddle-bags. Shyly he approached John Tanner and handed them to him. 'Señor Canasta is send these to you.'

'Thank you,' Tanner nodded. He found a half-dollar in his jeans and gave it to the kid who ran away happily.

Tanner did not look in the saddle-bags. He knew what he would find there, but not how much. He didn't care for the idea of being rewarded for bringing more heartbreak to Ben Canasta. He simply tied on the saddle-bags, stepped into the saddle on the back of the cantankerous buckskin and walked it out of the musty darkness of the barn into the clear sunlight of the desert morning. No one called out or tried to block his way.

Marshal Jack McGraw looked up unhappily when someone knocked on his door at the Knox jail. He wasn't in the mood for any new problems. Last night and this morning had been enough for awhile. The three Rader brothers had come to town last night intent on mischief, and they had finished up their party by trying to break up the Starlight Saloon. Not liking McGraw's interference with their

139

activities, they had come at him with every available weapon this side of guns. Thrown chairs, fists, booted feet and bottles. McGraw had managed to corral them with the help of a few citizens and gotten them penned up in the cells where they raged, cursed and vowed revenge into the early morning hours.

The Raders were all passed out now dreaming the peaceful dreams of the iniquitous while McGraw who had to stay up throughout the night, making reports and drinking half a pot of bitter black coffee was tired, sore and hungry. He glanced at the door and thought 'what now?' As he called out: 'Come in' in a grizzly baritone.

McGraw shouldn't have been surprised, the way troubles had been accumulating lately, still he was startled to see the last man he expected walk through the door. John Tanner walked toward his desk and stood there, hat in hands.

'You,' the town marshal said.

'I can't claim to be anybody else,' John answered with a faint smile. Behind the closed door leading to the jail cells one of the Rader brothers moaned in his sleep.

'What do you want, Tanner?' McGraw asked, rubbing his forehead with the heel of his hand.

'Justice,' John replied.

'Justice? If you've come to talk to me about your trial again. . . .'

'That's exactly what I've come to talk about,' Tanner interrupted.

'Look, Tanner,' McGraw said, tilting back in his chair. 'You were tried, convicted, sentenced in Matt Doyle's death.'

'That's the point,' Tanner said. The dubious marshal stroked his mustache and waited. 'I was convicted; I did do my time.' He leaned nearer to McGraw. 'That means that the law found me guilty – it also means that I've paid for my crime.'

'And?'

'And so I have come back to Knox. I know there are still some people who think I didn't do enough time, that I should have been strung up, but the law has been satisfied. This is what I came for,' he said as he unbuckled his gunbelt and placed his Colt on McGraw's desk. 'I mean to stay around Knox at least for a while. I don't want anyone to think I have come here to make trouble.'

'And?' McGraw probed, knowing there was more to this than had been said.

'And I expect the law to give me the same rights as any other free citizen – I do not wish to be harassed or beaten as occurred the last time I visited your town.'

'You're asking for my protection?' McGraw said with a frown.

'I'm asking that you provide me with the same measure of safety that you offer to any other citizen.'

'I see,' McGraw said with a puzzled expression, glancing at Tanner's surrendered weapon. 'You want me to baby-sit you.'

'I could take that Colt back and do it for myself,' Tanner said hotly, 'but you don't want that and I don't want it, McGraw.' Wearily he added, 'It's just that I don't want to do things that way any more.'

'All right,' McGraw said, holding up the palms of his hands. 'Maybe I just don't understand you, Tanner. Why would you want to come back to Knox where you were convicted and very nearly hanged?'

'I'm here mostly to buy a hat,' Tanner said.

'Oh, now it makes sense!' McGraw said sarcastically. 'What's the matter with the one you have?'

'Nothing. I want a woman's hat,' Tanner told the marshal.

'Why? Do you have a woman, Tanner?'

'I don't know. I won't know until after I buy the hat.'

'Tanner, I've had a long night, and you've got my head spinning,' McGraw said, using his hands as a vise against his skull. 'I need some sleep. Just go on your way, stay out of trouble, and I'll do my best to keep men off your back.'

As Tanner went out into the early morning streets of Knox, McGraw was already leaning back in his chair, eyes closed, trying his best to get some rest. The morning sky was faded purple, cool, with still a few stars lingering across the desert. There was almost no one about. The saloons were still open, but the men in them were only concluding an endurance test. There was no roistering, loud boasting, no laughter.

There were more cowboys and assorted desert rats sitting propped up against the alley walls or sound asleep on the sandy earth than there were inside the saloons. The defeated.

The restaurants, Tanner knew, would be open early, and now was a good time to go before the legion of John Barleycorn's army struggled to their feet and decided to put some solid food down before returning to the whiskey wars.

It was a hell of a town, Tanner decided as he walked the main street, feeling uncomfortable without the weight of his habitual handgun on his hip. Only the carcass of what its founders must have imagined. He tried not to glance at Candice Moore's hat shop as he passed it, but it was impossible. It showed him nothing but a blank face, innumerable questions, improbable scenarios. Had he been a fool to come back? Probably, but men will pursue dreams in the smallest of places.

There were only three men seated inside the restaurant as Tanner entered the warm, steaming, food-scented establishment. Two of these were speaking together at a far table, bearded prospectors, or that was the impression they gave. The other was a younger man sitting alone next to the wall, trying to drink the coffee he hoisted with trembling hands. A survivor – barely – of the night before.

A too-bright waitress approached Tanner and took his order. How did these women paste on that cheerfulness at this ungodly hour? It couldn't have been just for tips which must be meager at an hour like this, in a town such as this. He admired them for it, although they probably went home at night, stripped their boots from their tired feet and ranted at their husbands the rest of the time.

Tanner ate slowly, very slowly, watching the windows as the sun began to brighten them. He told himself it was still too early; the shops would not be open yet, but he knew in his heart that he was delaying the moment, afraid that this had all been just a foolish impulse.

It was still too early to go over to Candice Moore's

shop when he had finished eating. The restaurant was beginning to fill up now and it was obvious that they wanted his table, so Tanner rose, hoisted his saddle-bags and went out, leaving a few dollars on the table. Outside the sun was brilliant, the air still cool. The town was slowly beginning to stir. Tanner yawned widely. He was still weary and he did not want to present himself to Candice looking as he did, trail dusty and battered. He touched the bullet burn on his cheek and decided to clean up, sleep for a little while and then go over to the hat shop. Maybe a fresh appearance would make a better impression on Candice.

He took a room at the hotel and hiked up the stairs to it, his legs now feeling heavy, his body worn. Tanner sat on the bed, rose again and drew the curtains together to cut out some of the glare from the low sun and then began to consider his position. One of the first things he did was to open the buckles on the saddle-bags Ben Canasta had had delivered to him. He knew that they contained money, but after opening them his face froze with amazement. He dealt the bills on to the bed, stacked them and counted roughly.

He found at least a third of the money that he had recovered, and it was probably more than that. Half of the money, perhaps that the robbers had taken from Ben Canasta. Had he looked in the saddle-bags before leaving that C-bar-C, he would have returned it to Ben. It was certainly far too much of a reward. Now, of course, he would not return to the ranch. Ben had meant him to have it; the old man had considered Becky worth that much and he probably was not going to live long enough to spend the money anyway. Tanner silently thanked the man and tucked the money away.

He was already wishing that he had not been so cavalier in turning his Colt over to the marshal. After a short nap and a quick clean-up, he would march to the bank and deposit the money, hoping their safe was more theft-proof than Ben Canasta's had proven.

John only managed to rinse off his face before the bed summoned him and he crawled on to it, sleeping for three solid hours.

Awaking he found that there was no harsh sun glare in the room. The sun had risen high; the roof of the hotel now sheltered him from the sun. He peered at himself in the mirror. What he needed was a bath, a razor, a comb and some clean clothes. Rounding up all of those items would take longer than he wished to spare on this day. He needed to know how Candice Moore would welcome his return, and after all he had been in considerably worse shape when he had first met her.

He washed his face one more time, wiped back his hair and put on his Stetson. Then, retrieving his saddle-bags from beneath the bed he started out toward the bank that was one task he could not afford to put off. In the hallway he hesitated and then turned left, away from the lobby stairs. He had been to the Knox Hotel several times before this and knew there was a flight of stairs leading out the back of the building directly to the alley behind.

He opened the door on the landing, stepped out and closed it silently behind him. He proceeded down the flight of stairs toward the oily alleyway, saddle-bags over his shoulder.

And nearly walked into Wes Dalton.

TEN

The sallow, narrow gunman was leaning against the wall opposite the stairway. There was a gun in his hand, a smirk on his lips. John Tanner's hand dropped automatically to his thigh, but his accustomed holster was stuffed somewhere in the marshal's desk.

'Is that my money, Tanner?' Wes Dalton asked, nodding at the saddle-bags.

'No, it isn't,' Tanner said. 'How'd you find me, Dalton?'

'You've got no imagination – there wasn't anyplace else you could be. I checked the ponies in the stable this morning – I always do; I never know who might still be on my trail. And there it was, a big buckskin wearing the C-bar-C brand. The stable-hand described you. I knew you'd be in the hotel –

like I said, you've got no imagination.

'Now, if you don't mind, I'll have my money back, Tanner.'

'Who says this is it? Besides it was never your money. That was Ben Canasta's coin.'

'Oh, knock it off. Money changes hands every day. It gets traded back and forth. What's yours today is the bartender's or the boot maker's tomorrow. Wherever it came from, makes no difference – it's my money!'

'I don't see it that way,' John Tanner said.

'You'd better start seeing it that way,' Dalton said as he raised his Colt and eared back the hammer on the gun.

'You're taking a big chance, holding me up in broad daylight,' Tanner told him.

'In this town!' Dalton scoffed. 'You forget these are the folks that convicted you of murder two years ago then stewed because you didn't get strung up. Hell, they'd probably give me a medal for shooting you.'

It might have been true, John reflected. His reputation in Knox was lower than a snake's belly. Suddenly he didn't care any longer. About the C-bar-C, Becky's kidnapping, about Ben Canasta's money.

'Oh, hell,' he said in frustration, 'Take it!'

Tanner slipped the bags from his shoulder and stood holding them loosely in one hand. 'Take the money and get!'

'You'll be going along with me,' Wes Dalton said, taking a menacing step nearer.

'Why?'

'I've got an idea of what you are, Tanner. You're a man who just won't quit. You tracked me down once; you'd do it again. If I broke for Mexico, say, I'd look up one day to find you standing over me. You just don't give up.'

John considered trying to talk Dalton out of his notion, of explaining that his urge to do whatever was required to bring him and men like him, to justice had evaporated in the desert heat. But Dalton would have none of it – he had formed his plan and meant to stick to it. John also knew that if he rode out on to the desert with Wes Dalton nothing would ever be found of him but his bleached bones.

'Look, Dalton,' Tanner said reasonably. Then he hurled the saddle-bags into the man's face and broke toward the head of the alley. No shots followed, to John's surprise, but when he glanced back he saw that Dalton had not yet snapped out of his daze. No matter – he also saw that Dalton was now lining up his revolver for a killing shot.

Two shots rang out nearly simultaneously. As a bullet impacted the side wall of the hotel, sending a quiver of wood splinters into the side of John's face, he heard Wes Dalton whoop out in pain, turned to see Dalton up against the alley wall sag to a seated position, smoke still curling from the muzzle of his .44.

From the foot of the alley the big man appeared. Marshal Jack McGraw walked to where Dalton sat inertly, checked him briefly for signs of life, scooped up the saddle-bags and walked to where Tanner stood, hand to his face.

'Are these yours?' McGraw asked, holding out the saddle-bags to Tanner.

'Yes,' John panted, taking them.

'Let me see your face,' McGraw said gruffly, forcing Tanner's hand away from his cheek where dozens of splinters were embedded. 'That's not much,' McGraw said, holstering his pistol. 'We've got a pretty good young doctor in town now.'

'I know you do,' Tanner answered. 'Help me over to the hat shop.'

Jack McGraw who had been puzzling over Tanner's earlier remarks had come to understand what the younger man was getting at. He looped John's arm over his wide shoulders and the two men stumbled out into the sunlit main street of Knox

151

and made their way past curious eyes to the hat shop of Candice Moore.

'We can't have any more of this,' Candice said. She was sitting in a chair beside John Tanner who was reclined once again on her pink, canopied bed in the rear of her shop. She pulled one of the last splinters from his face with a pair of tweezers and dropped it into the basin she was balancing on her lap. 'Did you ever try to pluck a porcupine, John? I could give you some lessons now. There's a few smaller splinters that I'll have to go after with a needle, but those can wait.

'What happened this time?' Candice asked him, dropping the tweezers into the basin and placing it aside.

John tried to tell her the story, but there was so much he still did not understand that it was difficult. All the while Candice sat patiently listening, except for once when the tinkling of the front door bell called her out of the room. The dry breeze off the desert fluttered the ruffled pink curtains on the window, but the room was still comfortably cool. When Candice returned, Tanner finished his tale. She sat looking at him, a slight smile playing on her lips. Her dark hair reaching to her shoulders shifted slightly in the breeze.

152

'To tell you the truth,' he said with some frustration. 'I still don't really understand it all.'

'Of course you don't; you are a man,' Candice said.

'You mean you understand it?' he asked doubtfully.

'I think so – what was the root of the trouble between the two sisters?'

'Why, jealousy, I suppose '

Candice's smile deepened. 'I doubt it – it was money, John.'

'Money? They had plenty of money.'

'No. Ben Canasta had plenty of money. They were two young, adventurous women living out a life on the sterile solitude of the C-bar-C, far from entertainment of any kind, from shops and dances. I think they came up with the plan together – to take Ben Canasta's money, preferably after he had just finished a profitable cattle sale, which you say he had done, this time.'

'This time? You mean they had planned it earlier?'

'Oh, yes. I think Monique had taken up with Matt Doyle and convinced him to be a part of the plan. Unfortunately for Doyle, he was intrigued with Becky Canasta as well. He must have let something slip about Monique's plan – which did not now

153

include Becky.

'Becky taught Matt Doyle a lesson as well as Monique.'

'They were back where they had begun,' Tanner commented. Somehow his hand had stretched out and taken Candice's. She did not remove it.

'Yes, and if either woman had struck then it all would have seemed too coincidental, so they let the plan rest. Then they found out that you were to be released from prison in a few days. Maybe you had had the time in prison to think it over and realize what was up, or at least had a hint of what was going on at the C-bar-C. They had to act before you returned, or thought they did.

'Becky was further ahead on her planning this time. She had charmed Morgan Pride into helping her with the robbery and supposed kidnapping. Later, when Monique discovered that Becky had actually gone through with the plan, she became furious and convinced Ted Everly to go after them. If she promised him money or just more tainted kisses, I couldn't say.

'Anyway, that is the mess you were dropped into the middle of,' Candice said, leaning back in her chair, still holding John's hand. 'What do you think?'

'I think it makes as much sense as any other way

154

I can put it together, but nothing can be proved, and it doesn't matter anymore at this point. Both of them were such liars that anything is possible. Anyway,' he said with a shrug. 'It's all over now; that's all I care about.'

The bell over the front door jangled again, and before Candice could get up to go out, Marshal Jack McGraw strode in. He looked at Candice who dropped John's hand and then studied Tanner for a minute before saying:

'Your money's in the bank. Here's the deposit slip.'

John took it and looked at the verified amount of the deposit. 'Old Ben – I wish he hadn't done that.'

'I guess he figured you had earned it. No one forced him.'

'I know it – still I doubt that all of it has brought him any more happiness.'

'I guess not,' the marshal agreed. 'John, I've been talking to the men around town, trying to tell them what you explained to me – like it or not, you've done your time and the boys ought to leave you alone.'

'Thank you,' Tanner answered.

McGraw fumbled for a reply, did not find one, and simply started for the door. He paused in the doorway and looked around again, his eyes passing over Candice. 'I guess you'll be all right here for awhile.'

'Seems so.'

'Did you ever buy that hat you were looking for?' Jack McGraw asked.

'It looks like I won't be needing it after all,' John said and the marshal nodded. He might have smiled, but it was hard to tell. He was a man unused to such expressions.

'By the way, Tanner,' the marshal asked him. 'Wasn't there a man named Charlie Cox mixed up in all of this?'

'Yes, he was one of the robbers,' John told him.

'I thought so. It might interest you to know that he got himself arrested down in Las Palmas.'

'What happened?'

'Either Charlie was drunk or plain desperate. He tried to rob a Chinese laundry. Made off with seven dollars. But when he made his run out the rear of the building, he got himself tangled up in the clothes lines in the yard. Pulled nearly all of the clean laundry down. The Chinese went crazy and half beat him to death with sticks before the law could get there. He'll be spending a lot of time in jail.'

'That's the last of them, isn't it?' Candice asked.

'The last of them,' John answered quietly.

Still McGraw did not leave. He studied Tanner thoroughly and then asked:

'You didn't kill Matt Doyle, did you, Tanner?'

'No.'

'I didn't think so,' Marshal McGraw said, and he started toward the door of the hat shop.

'What was all that about a hat?' Candice asked, taking his hand again, this time holding it with both of hers. The sun was still bright in the window. It cast curving highlights in her dark hair. She was smiling with some secret knowledge. She was a knowing woman.

'Nothing,' John muttered lazily. 'I just thought. . . .'

'That you needed an excuse to come see me again?'

'Yes,' he had to admit.

'You didn't,' she replied softly. 'Are you going to stay around long, John?'

'Oh, I don't know,' he said, trying for indifference. 'I'd really like to settle down after the times I've had, but I can't reasonably expect someone to stay with me – a rambling man such as I have been.'

'Marriage? It's a large thought,' Candice said.

'Who said anything about marriage?' John Tanner asked.

'John,' Candice said, shaking her head in a

too-knowing way, 'why did you come here?'

She bent her head and kissed him softly. 'And you don't really need to buy a hat.'

The bell out front rang again and John felt like shouting at whoever it was to go away, but as Candice went out to greet the customer he rested his head back on the pink pillow and smiled at the empty day. Everything was done that could be done, except for planning for tomorrow. There are no pointless, lost trails in life. Each of them has a beginning and an end, some purpose.

John Tanner had found the end of his trail.

And its purpose.